Boggleswick

September 1939 and the
shadow of war

by Walt Oxer

First published in the United Kingdom in 2026 by
The Cloister House Press

Paperback ISBN 978-1-913460-94-5
eBook ISBN 978-1-913460-95-2

Also by Walt Oxer:

The Doonata trilogy:
A Gathering of Evil
Closing Time
River of Sorrow

Chicago Dolls

For Steve Chadwick, whose contribution to this story was of immense value.

Not forgetting Birgit Gurtier for her brilliant continuing cover designs.

CONTENTS

Part One

Part Two

Part Three

Part Four

PART ONE

PART ONE

Chapter 1

IT'S WAR

It was Sunday morning in the village of Boggleswick, North Yorkshire. A row of cottages curved in a half-moon around one side of the green, their gardens bright with the last of summer's flowers. At the centre of the green stood the granite war memorial, a brass statuette of a First World War soldier mounted on a four-sided pillar etched with the names of the fallen.

One name stood out, framed with carved laurels: Albert Bagley VC.

Inside cottage number 19, May Bagley was serving up an overcooked breakfast of sausages, eggs and tomatoes. Her son Horace eyed the meal with suspicion while his fiancée, Dora Seymore, tried not to laugh.

Horace waved a sausage at his mother and nudged Dora. 'Do you think these sausages could do with a few more minutes, Mother?'

May replied, 'They're cooked to perfection. Any longer and they'd be uneatable, Horace.'

'Oh, sorry, Mother... I was just thinking how they'd go better with these lovely eggs... err, I mean rubbery eggs.'

Dora giggled. May stabbed her fork in Horace's direction, shaking her head. 'Just like my Albert, his dad. Never satisfied.'

Horace gave the wireless a shake and cursed. 'Who the chuff bought a set of shite like this? It wants chuffing binning.'

Dora looked hurt. 'My daddy gave it you, Horace. For your birthday.'

May nodded. 'There, didn't I tell you, Dora love? My son doesn't appreciate anything given to him. Probably worked fine when your dad gave it him… but he'd have been fiddling with it. He's broken three of my clocks, one that Albert passed down from his great-great-grandfather.'

Horace laughed. 'Yes, a cuckoo clock. Must've had a dead bird in it. Never saw the bugger come out.'

May scowled. 'Because you were always messing with it.'

Dora shook her head. 'Woo, a dead cuckoo bird.'

Horace tossed his head at them. 'A wooden one!' He pointed at his mother. 'That silly bugger hung a string of millet over its exit hole.'

Suddenly the music cut out. An announcement crackled: the Prime Minister would address the nation from Downing Street. Neville Chamberlain's voice came through. Britain was at war with Germany.

A moment's silence followed. Then shouting outside drifted in through the open window of the Bagleys' cottage.

May, a stocky woman of forty-five, showed no concern at the cries of 'War! It is war!' Horace stared at the two women, shaking his head. At twenty-five, he had no intention of being dragged into a war. Not when he had Dora, the former village queen, childhood sweetheart, still as beautiful as ever at twenty-one, and their marriage ahead of them.

He thought of his father, whom he had never met: killed in the last days of the First World War. A hero, so they said. VC and all the rest.

He glanced at Dora, dangling a burnt sausage from her fork. For all her looks, she was a marble short in the brain department, a little far away at times.

Horace hurled the radio through the window, stamped his foot and shouted, making the women jump.

'What did I bloody well tell you, Mother, didn't I? That little kraut, Charlie Chaplin, would be chuffin' after bloody revenge, invading Poland.' He shook his head. 'They never could get over their loss in the bloody 1918 war.'

May inspected a sausage and glanced at Dora. 'Bit burnt. Left 'em in the oven too long. How's yours, Dora love?'

Horace shook his head again, staring at the ceiling.

'Bit burnt, bit burnt. We'll all be a bit burnt when Charlie sends us his chuffing bangers over.'

Suddenly the spout of a boiling kettle flew across the room and struck Horace on the neck. May looked confused.

'What's Charlie Chaplin doing making sausages, love? I thought he was a film star. He's English, y'know.'

Dora smiled and nodded. 'My dad likes him. Makes my dad laugh, he does.'

Horace strode to the table, rubbing his neck. May started giggling and set Dora off too. Horace glared, hands on hips.

'Doesn't take much to amuse little minds. Seeing a man struck with a bloody kettle spout and getting a blast to the ear from that chuffing wireless. Well, let me tell you pair of comedians, it's better than being struck with bullets and grenades. Because, my dears…'

He went to the mantel and picked up the photograph of his father.

'They took that man, but they ain't getting his son. They can keep their Victoria Crosses. Me, I don't want 'em. See, because my lovelies, Horace Bagley won't be going.' He sighed, staring at the photo. 'They're not taking me, Daddy.'

Dora walked over to the framed picture of the young man in

uniform, smiling with crossed eyes. She looked at it tenderly, then turned to May.

'He looks just like Horace. Double of his dad. He's got a faraway look in his eyes.'

Horace squinted at the photo and crossed his eyes.

May sniggered. 'Aye, one eye in York, t'other in Whitby.' She and Dora laughed uncontrollably. May clutched her apron. 'Oooh! Good job I've got me rubbers on. Shouldn't be laughing really. Lost my Albert in France.' She sighed. '1918. Died a hero, my man. Never even knew I was expecting Horace.'

Another sigh. Dora, with tears in her eyes, hugged May. 'Ohhh Mrs B, Mum.'

Horace fumed. 'Yes, and who were responsible, eh? Yer krauts. And who's chuffing at it again? Yer bloody krauts.' He clapped loudly. Dora hugged May tighter, startled by Horace's anger.

'Let me tell you now, as God is my judge. Them bastards took one Bagley, but they're not having another.' He jabbed a finger at his chest, sat down and threw a sausage at the bubbling kettle. 'So, one of you two fans of comedy gonna make a cup of tea?'

May rose, tapped Dora on the shoulder and whispered, 'Just like his father, cussing every second word. Don't know where they both got it from. Now my Albert's dad...' She nodded at Horace. 'His grandad was a lovely man. Church-going. Never missed a Sunday.'

Horace winked at Dora and smiled at May. 'Must've got it from your side of the family then. The Kelly wild bunch. Cousin Ned, wasn't he sentenced and sent to Australia? Well-known bank robber?'

May shook her head, then nodded at Dora. 'Here we go, recalling the past of the Kelly brigade.'

She tapped the table. 'My family were Irish. I come out of hard-working stock, I do. Half my family sailed off to America.

My father ended up in Yorkshire, a shaft sinker, a coal miner. My mother was a White Rose Yorkshire lass in full bloom.' She shrugged. 'All gone. They're all gone now.'

May walked over to the kettle, spluttering and coughing out vapour. 'Best make a cup of tea.'

Chapter 2
ARMSTRONG'S WORKS CANTEEN

Two weeks later

The factory canteen was crowded with men on their dinner break, seated in clusters at long tables. Some unwrapped lunchboxes while others ate the day's offering of pie and mash from the canteen counter. Every man had a large mug of tea. Above them, a freshly painted sign hung on the wall:

"Armstrong's ball bearings are keeping Britain's troops rolling."

Behind the counter, Dora and Thelma Ritson were busy pouring tea. Eric Swan, the works foreman and overlooker, sat alone at a table with a newspaper held open. His eyes flicked across the page but his ears twitched at every word from the men around him, who were talking about the war.

One old worker nodded his thanks as Thelma handed him a steaming mug. 'Aye, it were on t'wireless last night. Sending letters out, they are. Looks like conscription's a goer.'

Thelma smiled and nodded. 'One thing for certain, Norman, tha'll be safe at sixty. It's young guns they want.'

Suddenly the canteen doors banged open. Horace strode in

whistling. He called across to Dora, 'Make us a strong un, love, I'm gagging!'

Dora's eyes lit up as she waved back.

Eric peered over his newspaper and shouted, 'Here he is, Britain's secret weapon. He'll fill old Adolf's britches. That's if he's owt like his old man. What says you, Bagley?'

Horace nodded to the lads as he made for the counter. 'That you, Swanny? Thought you'd be on t'sick… what wi' all that hobbling and bloody limping tha's been doing these last two chuffing weeks.'

He took his tea from Dora, pecked her on the cheek and spotted Percy Rigby waving him over. As he walked past Eric, Horace began to limp exaggeratedly. The men roared with laughter and clapped, while Eric's face darkened.

'If tha had this arthritis I've got,' Eric snapped, 'tha'd know what bloody pain is.'

Horace winked. 'Aye, I'll bet old Chamberlain's call for conscripts has brought it on no end.' He nudged Percy. 'What says thee, Percy?'

Percy winked back. 'Could be right there, Horace old mate. Too bloody young for t'first war, too bloody old for t'second. That's Eric. Lucky bugger.'

Horace grabbed a broom leaning by the wall, swung it onto his shoulder and began to march around the canteen. Passing Eric, he turned the broom into a crutch and hobbled like an old cripple. The workers roared even louder, some doubling over in laughter.

'Can't you just see it, lads?' Horace shouted. 'Our Eric leading us into battle, hobbling in front, oversized balls in one hand, crutch in t'other!'

The men howled as Horace raised a hand for silence. 'Course, we could send a letter to t'War Office, tell 'em Armstrong's can't possibly join up without our beloved leader, Eric Attila Swan, marching us into battle. A man we'd follow to the very end!'

He pointed at Eric, whose face was thunderous.

The canteen echoed with cheers as Horace marched in circles, belting out Land of Hope and Glory.

Eric struggled to his feet, tucked the paper under his arm and hobbled to the door. He turned and waved his stick at them. 'Yeh can all bollocks, the bloody lot of yer!'

But before he could leave, the door flew open and Bobby Miller burst in, sending Eric sprawling.

Eric flailed on the floor, jabbing at Bobby with his stick. 'Silly young pillock! Done my leg in, he has. Ohhh, the bloody pain.' He reached out a hand for Bobby to help him up.

Bobby ignored him, panting breathlessly. 'Letters are out. All men eighteen to forty years. Postman Wooten's bag is bloody full to brim wi' em. Says every bugger's got one. Bloody hell, I'm just twenty. Still a baby… too young to die.'

Horace slung an arm round Bobby and laughed, shouting towards Eric, 'Hear that, Swanny? Up to forty years. Looks like tha's in!'

Chapter 3

THE CONSCRIPTS

One week later

Inside Boggleswick's village hall, Captain Pete John Caruthers MD paced the small inner office while his sergeant major, Colin Kennedy, looked on and shook his head. The makeshift surgery looked like something out of the eighteenth century: Caruthers wore a white coat with a stethoscope slung round his neck, two bales of straw with a blanket served as an examination table, and a side table displayed a grim selection of surgical instruments. An eye chart was tacked to the wall.

Caruthers waved his arms in exasperation. 'What I'd like to know is, who decked out this ruddy surgery?' He jabbed a finger at the straw before picking up an ancient horse tooth extractor and tossing it across the room. 'Ruddy bundles of hay, and those bloody medieval instruments of torture over there. They told me to bring nothing surgical, that I'd only need my stethoscope. I ask you, Sergeant Major, is someone taking the piss? Trying to pull Peter John's plonker?'

Kennedy coughed. 'Err, this whole village is full of idiots if you ask me, Sir. Local vet supplied the, err… instruments of torture. Every man under fifty's out there, Sir.' He shook his head. 'Bandaged up t'bolocks they are, sitting out there. With their bandages and ruddy crutches they look like they've just been in a war. We've some sorting to do, that's for sure. A long day ahead, Sir.'

Caruthers nodded. 'Well let's get started. Wheel them in, Sergeant Major.'

Kennedy opened the door and glanced down at his list. 'Tobias Flint!'

In the main hall the benches were filled with men, many swathed in suspicious bandages. Amid the chatter Tobias Flint leapt up. He was bare of bandages and marched proudly past a surprised Kennedy into the surgery. He came smartly to attention before the doctor's desk and saluted.

Caruthers smiled. 'At ease, lad. You're not in uniform yet, but I hope all to follow will show as much spirit as you. Flint, isn't it?'

Tobias stood tall and winked. 'Can't wait to get at 'em, Sir. The Hun. Let's get this over with.'

Caruthers patted his shoulder. 'Army needs men like you, Flint. Let's give your chest, heart and lungs the once-over.' He opened Tobias's shirt and set the stethoscope to his chest.

Tobias flinched. 'Sorry, bit cold that, Doc.'

'Nothing amiss,' Caruthers muttered. 'Strong as a lady's knicker elastic. Now drop your trousers, turn your head right, and give me a cough.'

Tobias obeyed. Caruthers frowned. 'Now what have we here, Flint?'

'Oh, that's nowt, Sir. Me support belt. Got it when I strained misen lifting the anvil. Don't stop me running or owt. I'm the village blacksmith.'

Caruthers tutted. 'I'm afraid it is something. Can't have you fighting the enemy wearing that belt. Sergeant Major. M.E.'

Tobias blinked. 'M.E.? What's that, Doc?'

'Medical exempt. Looks like home guard for you.'

Tobias's shoulders slumped. Kennedy ushered him out with a gentle pat.

In the hall all eyes turned as Tobias re-emerged, crestfallen.

'Hey Toby,' Horace called, 'you passed, yeh? Didn't fail surely?'

Tobias kicked at a bench. 'Bloody failed. Strongest man in the chuffin' village. Failed! Medical exempt, he says. When the army don't want yeh, nobody does.' He thumped the wall, sending plaster dust down.

Percy Rigby slung an arm round him. 'That's a cruel blow, Tobe. You looked fitter than any of us. What did they fail you on?'

Tobias tugged his waistband. 'This bloody belt. Told him I'd worn it fifteen years. M.E., he says. Oh, I could cry.'

Percy leaned close. 'Follow me, Tobe. I've an idea.'

He led Tobias to the back toilets, ushered him into the ladies'. Tobias tugged at his sleeve. 'Percy, we can't go in here!'

'We're alright, no women here today. Listen. You're going in the next cubicle. Take off that belt and toss it over. I'll wear it. When they see it, I'll get M.E. same as you. Then I'll give it you back. Save me life, Tobe.'

Tobias looked worried. 'Tha sure it'll work?'

Percy grinned and hugged him. 'Chuffing well worked for thee, didn't it? Now quick, before they call me name.'

Moments later Percy and Tobias returned. Tobias muttered, 'Remember, I know nowt about this. Bring it to me house after, and for God's sake don't lose it.' He shook his head and left.

The surgery door burst open. Bobby Miller stumbled out, shoved by an angry Kennedy. 'Don't think you can fool the army, Miller. Your pains'll increase when I get you back at barracks, that I promise.'

He turned to the trembling men. 'Next! Eric Swan!'

Caruthers rubbed his hands as Kennedy called the name. 'Let's hope we capture a few more Flints, eh Sergeant Major?'

Kennedy muttered, 'Hope's the word, Sir.'

Eric entered on crutches, his knee heavily bandaged. Caruthers tapped it with his crop. 'Seems to be trouble here, Swan. Painful, I imagine?'

'Aye, killing me, Doc. Arthritis. Want to chop me leg off, I do.'

Caruthers raised a brow. 'Funny. I saw you leaving the Red Lion last night. Without crutches. We don't appreciate liars, do we, Sergeant Major?'

Eric stammered. 'Err… good days and bad uns. Drink sets it off, if tha knows what I mean, Doc.'

Caruthers turned to Kennedy and whispered. Kennedy nodded gravely.

'Well then,' Caruthers said, 'we think it best to do a double leg amputation. Can't bear to see a man in pain. Least I can do.'

Eric paled. 'Not so fast, Doc! Don't you think army exercise'll do me good? Pain's going already.'

Caruthers patted his back. 'That's the spirit. Born leader, Swan. Army life will suit you. Now get the blood circulating, by getting out of my ruddy sight.'

He slapped his crop on the straw bed. 'Send in the next ruddy actor, Sergeant Major.'

Kennedy shoved Eric aside and barked, 'Next! Horace Bagley!'

Horace barged in, knocking Eric into the doorframe and sending his crutches sprawling. Kennedy jammed them back under Eric's arms with a growl. 'Stop wasting the army's time, lad.'

Caruthers eyed Horace. 'Now here's a fit recruit. No bandages. A born soldier, Sergeant Major.'

Kennedy grinned. 'Indeed, Sir.'

Horace pulled jam-ja- thick glasses from his pocket and put them on. 'That's better. Can't see a bloody thing without 'em.'

Caruthers led him to the eye chart. 'Cover your left eye and read the chart top to bottom.'

Horace scratched his chin. 'Forgot to tell thee, Doc. Can't read. I'll give it a go though. First letter... C for khaki?'

Caruthers glared. 'And the next, Bagley, is N – for knuckles, which you'll get if you don't stop playing silly buggers.'

Horace sighed. 'Told thee I couldn't read. Don't tha believe me?'

Caruthers steered him to the window. 'See that hill beyond the church tower?'

Horace spat on his glasses, wiped them on Caruthers's smock and squinted. 'That blurred thing? Used to go mushrooming there.'

'Never mind the mushrooms. If there was a fat black crow on that tower, could you shoot it from here?'

'What, wi' me catapult?'

Caruthers stamped his foot. 'No, lad, not with a ruddy catapult! With a .303 rifle!'

Horace scratched his chin. 'No chance, Doc.'

Caruthers shouted in his ear. 'What about ten fat crows? Fifty? A thousand?'

Horace winced. 'No need to shout, Doc. I'm short-sighted, not chuffing deaf.'

Caruthers reddened but forced a smile. 'What about ten thousand crows? Could you hit one at two hundred yards?'

Horace shrugged. 'I'd try.'

'That's good. Welcome to the King's army, lad. The army loves a trier.'

Horace looked horrified. 'But—'

'Next, Sergeant Major!'

Kennedy pushed him out with a smirk. 'Bring your ruddy catapult, Bagley. You'll need it when you meet them German Goliaths.'

'Percival Rigby!' he bellowed.

Percy passed Horace in the doorway and approached Caruthers with a broad grin.

Caruthers shook his hand. 'Good to see a man with a smile. I hope you can read?'

Percy winked. 'I'll help thee all I can, Doc.'

Caruthers smirked. 'Which one are you? Flanagan or Allen?'

'Just Rigby, Doc. Call me Percy if tha likes.'

'Then call me Peter. Shall I order us some tea? Won't mind if I include the RSM? But first, unbutton that shirt.' He breathed on the stethoscope. 'Don't want to put it cold on your chest.'

Percy nodded. 'Still a bit cold, Doc.'

'Strong lungs, good heart,' Caruthers said. 'Now drop those trousers and cough.'

He spotted the support belt. 'Well, well, Sergeant Major. Another one.'

Kennedy peered. 'Looks like a rupture support, Sir.'

Percy nodded. 'Had it seventeen years. Lifting anvils, heavy iron. Did me in. Belt keeps me going.'

Caruthers laughed. 'This village has more blacksmiths than Newmarket! Seventeen years you've worn it, eh?'

'Give or take,' Percy shrugged.

'Then it's settled. Sergeant Major, our friend Percy's M.E.'

Percy yelped. 'Medical exempt? You're not taking me? I'm upset, I am!'

Caruthers winked. 'You misunderstood, lad. Not medical exempt. Middle East. If you can wear a rupture belt back to front for seventeen years, you can ride a camel in the desert. Off you go. And you forgot to take Tobias Flint's name from the belt. Next!'

Chapter 4

THE SUPPLY LORRY

Six weeks later

Horace, Percy and Bobby were now privates in the King's colours. To their dismay, Eric Swan had somehow been made a corporal, and he was making life as hard as possible, especially for Horace. The four of them were taking a lorry of supplies from Yorkshire to Dover, where a cargo vessel waited.

Eric drove south on a cold, misty March night. Percy and Bobby sat beside him in the cab, while Horace had been banished to the rear.

The army lorry rattled along a lonely country road. Bobby blew into his hands and rubbed them together. 'It's bloody cold in here. Can't we stop for a cuppa, Eric?'

Percy nodded eagerly. 'Good idea, Bob. Nice cup of Rosie Lee and a fag. Are we stopping or what, Eric?'

Eric tapped his stripes. 'That's Corporal Swan to you pair of scumbags. You should think yourselves lucky you're not sat in the back with Bagley. Bet he's bloody freezing, wanting a brew.' He nudged Bobby and laughed wildly. 'Hope he's got his long johns on. I'll give him what-for when we get back. Our Eric leading you into battle, lads!' He shook his shoulder to flash the

17

stripes at them. 'Corporal Swan, leading you. And pushing you. Hear me, Bagley? You'll wish you were never born when your leader's finished with you!'

Percy and Bobby exchanged a nervous glance. Eric's eyes blazed as he muttered to himself. 'Petitions, bloody petitions. Letters to t'War Office. Can't fool old Eric. They'll bloody pay. All the scumbags will pay!'

In the back, Horace sat on a box marked GRENADES, clutching a blanket around his shoulders. The canvas cover flapped as he bounced with the lorry's jolts, cigarette hanging from his lips. He could hear Eric's ranting through the boards. When the lorry braked sharply, Horace was thrown forward. He pulled back the canvas flap and peered out.

They'd pulled into the car park of a roadside inn, The Haymakers. Only a couple of bicycles leaned against the wall.

Eric jumped down first, with Percy and Bobby hopping out, shivering and stamping to keep warm.

'Half an hour, no more,' Eric barked. 'We've a tide to catch. That ship won't wait. If we're late, it's your bollocks, not mine.'

Horace came round from the back, still smoking, rubbing his gloved hands. Percy grinned when he saw him. 'Gis us a fag, Horace. I'm gagging.'

Horace pulled a packet from his breast pocket and passed it over. 'Shouldn't be gagging, mate. Thousands of cigs in t'back. Got gloves too, if you've none.'

Eric stepped forward and knocked the packet to the ground. 'Tha'll not take fags off our fighting men. You'll get your supply when we reach France.' He scooped up the cigarettes and stuffed them into his own pocket.

Bobby stamped his feet. 'It's a hot drink I want. Can we go in, Eric— err, Corporal?'

Horace nodded. 'Second that, Bobby. Too bloody cold to be standing out here.'

He made for the inn door, but Eric snapped, 'And where do

you think you're going, Bagley? Don't think for one minute you're stepping inside. Not you. My bloody Willy Shakespeare, writing petitions to t'War Office. You'll wish you'd never learnt to write. You'll stay right here, guarding the supplies. Wouldn't want them falling into unwelcome hands, would we, Bagley?'

He sneered, then winked at Percy and Bobby. 'Hot tea. Hot toddy, more like. As for you two shits, you can join him if you like.'

Percy whispered to Horace, 'I'll bring thee one out soon as I get the chance, mate.'

Left behind, Horace climbed into the cab, stamping his feet and rubbing his arms. Even with the windows shut, he could hear the laughter spilling from the inn. He jammed his fingers in his ears, then lay down across the bench.

His eyes caught the lorry key in the ignition, the engine left running. He sat up.

'Am I thinking what I'm thinking?' he muttered. 'One turn and away from all this shite. Horace Willy Shakespeare Bagley, free man.' He paused. 'Naah.'

He curled up again and drifted into uneasy sleep.

Dreams came: trench warfare, men forced over the top by Eric Swan, bodies falling, shells exploding. Dora running on a beach, laughing as the tide chased her feet.

Horace woke with a start. Eric's laughter still echoed in his head. He stared at the ignition, then smiled.

'No contest. Tha can keep thee bloody tea, Swanny.'

He twisted the key, shouted and ground the gears. With a salute to the steamed-up inn window where a hand wiped away condensation, Horace swung the lorry round and drove out of the car park. At the crossroads he turned north, following the sign for the A1.

Chapter 5

THE VILLAGE GREEN, BOGGLESWICK

It was midnight and Horace, driving the stolen army lorry without lights, pulled up alongside Boggleswick Green's war memorial. He climbed out of the cab, stood still listening, then crept off towards the cottages. They were all in darkness. He walked slowly round to the backs of them via a side pathway, stopped at a gate and listened. Satisfied, he opened it and entered the garden of Number 16. Passing a large fish pond, he headed towards the potting shed and carefully picked up a ladder, which he carried and propped beneath an upstairs window. He climbed it.

Meanwhile Jack Seymore, on Home Guard duty in uniform with three sergeant's stripes, was inspecting the parked army vehicle. He walked around it, checking the tyres, then stopped at the door and peered inside, scratching his head. He moved on, taking the path that led to the back of the cottages. Jack froze when he saw movement at the rear of his own cottage, Number 16. Taking a truncheon from his belt, he crept closer. His eyes widened at the sight of a ladder propped up to his daughter's bedroom window, with a figure climbing it.

Horace tapped lightly at Dora's window, hooting like an owl.

'Oo ow, oooow, oooow.'

The bedroom curtain opened. Dora lifted the window, holding a chamber pot in her hand. She hurled it at the figure on the ladder. Horace ducked. The pot, along with its contents, landed squarely on Jack's head just as he was about to surprise Horace. The pot stuck fast, and Jack, struggling, tumbled into the pond.

Horace, panicking, hissed up at the window: 'Dora, Dora, it's me, love! Horace!'

'Horace? Horace! What's going on? What on earth's up wi' yeh?' she gasped.

Horace squeezed her hand. 'Can't explain now. Get dressed, quick as you can. Meet me at your front door, and bloody hurry. Pack some clothes in a suitcase, like we're going on holiday. Hurry, love, please hurry.'

'Can I tell me mum we're going on holiday?' Dora asked.

'No, bloody hell. Don't tell anyone.'

Dora pointed down to the pond with a squeak. 'Whooo's that? Whoooo's that?'

Horace looked down at the struggling Jack, still half in the water with the pot wedged tight on his head. Alarm flashed across Horace's face.

'It... err... looks like your dad. What's he bloody doing?' He sighed. 'Dora, love, come on, we've got to go. Please hurry.'

Dora blew him a kiss and slammed the window.

'Bloody hell, Dora, you'll wake the whole chuffing street,' Horace muttered, scurrying down the ladder. He shoved past Jack, knocking him back into the pond, and raced to the front door.

Dora, half dressed and struggling with a suitcase, stumbled out. Horace snatched the case, hurried her to the lorry, and threw it into the back. He gave her a quick kiss, lifted her gently into the cab, and scrambled in after her. With headlights blazing, he sped the lorry out of the village.

*

Meanwhile, at the rear of the cottages, Babs Seymore – Jack's wife and Dora's mother – had opened her bedroom window after hearing the commotion. At fifty she was still a striking woman, with an hourglass figure and no shortage of admirers, though Jack knew nothing of that.

Babs called down to the chamber-potted figure: 'What the chuffin' hell's going on? Is that you, Jack?'

Jack, snarling and cursing, shouted back: 'Aye! Get down here and get this bloody Jerry off me!'

Babs shrieked hysterically: 'Help! Help! Bloody Germans are here! Help me! They've got Jack!' She yelled louder still. 'Get the police, the bloody army! Jerrys have got our Jack!'

Lights flicked on across the cottages as Babs's cries echoed through the night. Windows opened.

'Germans? Can't bloody see 'em! What's all this chuffin' commotion?' one neighbour yelled. 'I need my bloody rest, I'm up at six, while you lot are snoring. So shut it!'

Another woman's voice cried out: 'Bloody Jerrys? Ain't took 'em long. God help us!'

A man grumbled angrily: 'God help me if I don't get to work. I've just got back after being off sick. If I'm late, I'll get the chuffin' sack. They really piss me off, them Jerrys. Really piss me off.'

Chapter 6
CRASH, BANG, WALLOP

The army lorry left the village at top speed, heading north into open country. Horace was at the wheel, constantly checking the mirrors. Dora sat beside him, frightened, glaring at him and waiting for some kind of explanation for his strange behaviour.

In the distance, headlights appeared on the undulating road, then vanished, then reappeared, steadily drawing closer. Horace grew alarmed. He shouted to Dora, 'Hold tight, love! Hang on to me!'

He wrenched the wheel sharply right, sending the lorry off the road and into a wooded area. The cab bounced and swayed violently, throwing Horace and Dora from side to side. Horace gripped the wheel with all his strength, trying to steady it.

Dora screamed, 'Horace, I'm going to be sick! Stop it! Pull up, pleaseeee Horace!'

But Horace was determined to get as far from the road as possible, from whatever danger lay behind those lights. He steered hard through the trees, crunching through undergrowth, branches cracking against the cab. He forced a smile at Dora, trying to reassure her.

'Keep with me, love. Just a little bit more. I'll find a clearing and we'll stop, that's a promise.'

He kissed her cheek and, taking one hand off the wheel, pulled her into a hug.

The lorry jolted and bucked as branches thrashed the windows and doors. Then, with a violent surge, the whole cab lurched. Horace grabbed Dora and pulled her close.

She clung to him and screamed, 'Weeerrre going over! Help!'

The lorry toppled into a deep ditch.

Silence followed, broken only by the hiss of the busted radiator and the whirring spin of a wheel. Inside the upturned cab, Horace and Dora lay motionless.

Chapter 7

THE LONG WALK HOME

On a desolate country road, after midnight, it was cold, misty and wet. Eric marched like a madman, Percy and Bobby trailing a little way behind.

He stopped suddenly and turned on them, shouting. 'I'll bloody well give you "let's stop for a cuppa tea, Eric." You've got Eric right in't shit, bloody deep in. The later we're back to barracks, the harder it's gonna be. Kennedy's going to come down on stupid me. Yes, me!'

He cried out into the night, 'I was in charge of you, and that nutter Bagley. He's gone and done it this time. Firing squad for him, my lovelies. And I hope they give me the job of putting the bullets into his cowardly heart.'

Percy whispered to Bobby, 'I was gonna ask him for a break. We can't keep pace with him. He's like a man possessed. And Horace... I can't believe it.'

Bobby shook his head. 'Can't say I blame Horace, Percy. Eric's been riding him hard ever since we joined up. Fact is, we know Horace didn't send any petition to t'War Office.' He nodded towards Eric. 'But try convincing that man.'

Percy winked. 'If truth ever comes out, I'd lay money it was his wife who sent off the petition.'

Bobby's mouth fell open. 'What! Tha means Eric's missus? Nay, she wouldn't do that… would she?'

Percy nudged him. 'Wouldn't thar, if tha were married to Eric?'

Eric spun round, eyes narrowed. 'What you two bastards on about, eh? I can hear you mumbling. Hope you're not talking about me.'

Percy shook his head quickly. 'Err, no. We were just saying… isn't it time we had a break, Eric? We've been walking for hours.'

Eric snarled. 'Break? The only break you two'll get is when I break your chuffin' legs. Now get moving, because the way Eric's feeling, I just might do it.'

He picked up a broken tree branch and, staring at them, snapped it clean in half. Percy and Bobby hurried forward at a brisk pace.

Bobby muttered, 'If tha'd let us in for a drink, we wouldn't be in this mess. And trying to steal two bicycles – that was some mistake. Luckily for us, phoning the barracks got us off. Sorry, Corporal, but it's all thy fault.'

Eric snarled. 'Bagley's fault, not Eric's!'

Chapter 8

BERTIE THE HERMIT

In a deep cave hidden within Bogie Wood – the place locals whispered about as the haunt of the dreaded Wolf Man – Horace and Dora stirred. The cave was a clutter of oddments, a poor man's Aladdin's cave. A bath stuffed with straw and blankets. A great British Railways clock frozen forever at two-fifteen. Boxes, crates, suitcases, handbags. Chairs with their horsehair bursting out. Old carpets, scraps and countless bits and pieces. Oil lamps flickered beside a crackling wood fire. From a crack in the ceiling, water dripped steadily into an overflowing oak cask.

Horace lay by the fire, grimacing as he rubbed his shoulder. With a groan he sat up, glanced at Dora beside him and bent down to feel her breath. Relieved she was alive, he shook her gently.

'Come on, sweetheart. Come on, Dora love.'

She coughed, rolled over and blinked at him. He reached to comfort her … and froze. A rifle barrel was pressed into his neck.

There was silence, broken only by Horace's gasp. 'Swanny? That you? Go on then, in the back, aye, I'd expect that from thee. Just up thy street, that. Go on then, what's tha waiting for?'

A rough, elderly voice asked, 'Thar Jerry German? … Eh? You Germany man? I kill Germany man.'

Horace mouthed the word "German," confused. 'Who the chuff? Been on't piss or what?'

The voice pressed. 'She Germany woman, eh?'

Horace snapped, 'Now listen here, you hater of the German race. I'm not a chuffing German.' He pointed at Dora. 'She's not a Jerry. We're bloody English. Not Jocks, Taffs or Paddies. Yorkshire!'

'You tell truth? No lie to Bertie?'

Horace sighed. 'I'm absolutely certain. And if the truth be known, you sound more bloody German than me.'

The barrel lifted from his neck. Horace turned slowly.

Before him stood a Robinson Crusoe figure: a little man of fifty who looked a hundred. Long hair, a matted beard. A child's pop-gun rifle in hand. A lady's blue coat fastened with a brooch, trousers halfway up his shins, odd football stockings and on his feet, a pair of miners' pit boots ten sizes too big.

Horace rubbed his eyes. 'What the—?'

The man scuttled towards Dora, prodding her with the toy rifle. He squinted at Horace. 'She dreaded, her?'

'No, she's not bloody dead,' Horace barked. 'But she bloody well will be if you don't stop waving that silly gun at her.'

The stranger tapped his chest. 'Me Bertie. Not German. I not like Germans. They kill my friend. War long time gone.'

Horace nodded. 'Aye, tha's not alone. Truth is, Bertie boy, I've probably more reason to hate the bastards than thee.' He showed his identity tags. 'K.O.Y.L.I. British soldier. Boggleswick. Yorkshireman. King's Own.'

He spread his arms wide. 'Like here. Yorkshire. And that's Dora, my wife. My Yorkshire wife.'

Bertie cocked his head, cross-eyed. He pointed around the cave. 'This my home. Bertie's home. You go find home. This Bertie's home.'

Dora, blinking awake, sat up. 'Who you talking to, love? Who's there?'

When she saw Bertie she screamed. Horace rushed to calm her.

'Hush, love. It's alright. It's only Bertie. We're in his home.'

Bertie grinned, showing blackened teeth. Dora shuddered at the sight of the cave.

'But it's a cave, Horace. Not a home. Not like my mum's. Where are we?'

'Not far,' Horace admitted. 'Just outside t'village. In Bogie Wood.'

Her eyes widened. 'The Wolf Man's wood? Owww, Horace, I'm scared!'

She pointed at Bertie. 'Is he a rag-and-bone man?'

'No love. He's Bertie. Harmless, poor old soul. Probably got no family. Nobody loves him. Forced to live off the land any way he can.'

Bertie hung his head sadly. Horace sighed. 'That's what we'll have to do, till this war ends. They said by Christmas. Looks like we'll be spending it with Bertie.' He turned to their host. 'That's if he'll let us stay.'

Dora frowned. 'Can't we stay at your mum's, Horace?'

'No way. They'd have me shot in an instant. I need time to think. We can't stay here forever, it's not fair on Bertie. We weren't born to live like this. But for now, love, it's all we've got.'

At the mention of war, Bertie went wild, hopping and yelling. 'War! War! Kill Jerry! I kill Germans!'

Horace grabbed his shoulder. 'Aye, Bertie, we're at war. Them Germans are at it again. And them clothes of yours want a good wash.'

'Language, Horace,' Dora scolded. 'Bertie don't cuss and swear.'

'No he don't,' Horace muttered, 'but he bloody well would if he knew what was going on in this world.'

He faced Bertie. 'Look, me old son. Dora and I, we're on the run. Bad men are after us. They'll prison us, maybe shoot us. I'm asking you, let us stay. Be our friend.'

He grimaced, spreading his arms. 'In… your lovely home. Just for a while, till I work something out.'

Bertie blinked and thought. Horace tried to sweeten the deal. 'There's food, cigarettes, blankets, grenades, everything in that lorry.'

Bertie's face lit. 'Bertie got food. Lots of food. Cigs. Blankets. Bertie keep warm when snow comes.'

He lifted a lantern and led them to an alcove stacked to the roof with the lorry's supplies.

Horace whistled. 'Bloody hell, Dora. Bertie's some boy. Got the army's supplies in here.' He nodded at Bertie. 'You don't miss a trick, lad. Just keep a flame off those ammo boxes or we'll all be blown to kingdom come.'

Dora whispered, 'Is Bertie going to let us stay then, Horace?'

Bertie shrugged, scratched his beard, then nodded.

Horace moved to hug him, but stopped when a spider crawled from Bertie's beard. Bertie plucked it free and calmly ate it. Horace gagged and forced a smile. 'Err… thanks, Bertie. That's settled then. I'll make us a bed. Plenty of blankets, courtesy of His Majesty's army.'

'I'm dizzy,' Dora murmured. 'Hungry, too.'

'Rest, love. I'll make us a meal. Want a drink of water?'

Before he'd finished, Bertie rushed up with a mug. Horace lifted it to Dora's lips, but she recoiled. Inside, a goldfish swam in circles.

'Err, no thank you, Bertie. I'm alright for now,' Dora said, forcing a smile.

Horace showed him the cup. 'This water's alright, Bertie? Only there's a fish in it.'

Quick as a flash Bertie snatched it back. 'Wrong cup. This Bertie's little friend. Little fishy Willie.'

As Horace gathered bedding, he noticed photographs pinned to a "Beware of the Bull" sign. He lifted one, stared and went pale.

'Horace, what's wrong?' Dora asked.

He turned to Bertie, holding up the photo. 'Bertie… who's this?'

Bertie clutched it to his chest, kissing it. 'This Bertie's girl. Mine. My girl.'

'Show Dora,' Horace said quietly.

Reluctantly Bertie handed it over. Horace held a lamp high. Dora stared, bewildered.

'Horace… why's Bertie got a photo of your mum?'

Horace lifted the lamp to Bertie's face. In the light, his eyes crossed comically.

Horace gasped. 'Dad? Daddy… is that you?'

Chapter 9
THE BARRACKS

The following day three worn-out soldiers – Eric, Percy and Bobby – sat locked in the holding cell of the army barracks. Their feet were in bowls of water, boots and socks discarded nearby, trousers rolled past their knees. Percy and Bobby were down to vests, while Eric still wore his corporal's jacket.

The cell door unlocked. Percy whispered to Bobby, 'Is it snap time already? I'm famished. I could eat an elephant.'

The door suddenly flew open. In marched Sergeant Major Kennedy, closely followed by Colonel James Harris.

'On your ruddy feet now!' Kennedy barked. 'Commanding Officer in attendance! Jump to it! Attentions!'

The three struggled up, stamping their feet into the water bowls in their effort to come to attention. Water splashed across the floor, onto the officers' boots and trousers. Harris shook his head at the mess as Kennedy bent to wipe at his colonel's shoes.

Kennedy snarled, 'Corporal Swan, Privates Rigby and Miller, Sir.'

Harris walked over to Eric and violently tore the stripes from one sleeve, then the other. Eric ground his teeth, tears welling. Harris winked at Kennedy. 'Private Swan, Sergeant Major.

Private.' He leaned nose to nose with Eric. 'Didn't get to wear those stripes long now, did we, Swan?'

Eric stammered, 'No, Sir. No.'

Harris shook his head at each man in turn. He tutted. 'So what have we here? I'll ruddy well tell you. The ruddy Three Stooges, Sergeant Major. Curly, Larry and Mo, in my regiment!'

He shouted in their faces. 'While their comrades are up to their necks in blood and bullets, dying for want of a fag and a last cup of ruddy tea – the sort they give out in the Haymakers – you three are making fools of yourselves!'

He slammed his crop down on a side table. 'But Sergeant Major, they are not going to get that last fag. That last cup of tea. Why? Did I hear someone ask why?'

He turned on Eric and stared.

Eric croaked, 'Wh... who, Sir?'

Harris screamed, jabbing him in the chest. 'Because while the three ruddy Stooges were having their hot toddies, Bagley was making off with a lorry load of ruddy army supplies, that's why!'

Eric clenched his fists, teeth grinding. Harris circled them, tapping his crop against his palm. Kennedy glared, hatred plain on his face. As he bent to brush water from his boots he used a table for support. Harris, spinning in anger, slammed the crop down – straight onto Kennedy's fingers.

Kennedy yelped, shoved Bobby aside and plunged his hand into one of the water bowls, his face showing relief as the pain eased.

Harris loomed nose to nose with Eric again. His voice dropped. 'To lose an army supply lorry to the enemy is bad enough.' He raised it, louder. 'But to lose it before it even reached the docks, before it left the safety of our shores,' his voice now thundered, 'it's ruddy unheard of!'

He turned his back. Eric, sweating, wiped his brow. Kennedy barked into his ear, 'Keep that hand down by your side, Swan, or the colonel will chop it off. Won't you, Sir?'

Harris swung round again and paced slowly before them. 'So what are we going to do, eh?'

Eric tried to smile. 'Err, well—'

'Don't you dare speak while the CO is talking!' Kennedy roared. 'Keep that mouth shut!' He pulled his hand from the bowl, sucked his fingers and blew on them.

Harris continued pacing. 'The Brigadier himself – yes, the Brigadier – has instructed me, against my better judgement, to give you clowns a chance to redeem yourselves. To bring back some shred of honour to this regiment, which has become the laughing stock of the British Army.'

He snarled. 'You will leave for the village of Boggleswick, the last known sighting of our friend Bagley. You will take whatever action is necessary to return that vehicle and its contents, and capture Bagley.'

He banged his crop repeatedly on the table, Kennedy now keeping his hands firmly behind his back.

'I want that lorry, and I want that traitor back here. Do I make myself clear?'

The three privates shouted in unison, 'Sir!'

PART TWO

Part Two

Chapter 10
THE SEARCH

It was a bright sunny morning. In the cave Horace was bending and stretching his arm while Dora fiddled with a radio transmitter that gave out high-pitched whistles mixed with voices in a foreign tongue.

Dora, frustrated, muttered, 'Worse than your mum's, this is.'

Horace grinned. 'Best you check it ain't me mum's, love. Wouldn't surprise me one bit.' He waved his arms. 'No wonder that postman of ours is always knackered. His chuffing bike's here, over in the corner. Turn that machine off, love. Man can't think wi' that blaring out. Wouldn't be so bad if I could chuffing understand what they're saying.'

Dora turned the dial. Bertie hummed while stirring a large cooking pot over the fire, using a snapped-off twig as a spoon. He pointed at the British Railways clock.

'Yum yum. Quarter past two.'

Horace scowled. 'So tha can tell time, Father. My mother, twenty-five bloody years. God help us.'

Before he could say more, a broken English voice came from the transmitter:

'Come in, Tommy. This is Gdansk calling you. Where are you? Tommy, help us. Tommy, this is Gdansk, Poland. Help us.'

Horace strode to the set and switched it off. 'Wouldn't you like to know, mate? It's us that could do wi' some chuffin' help. Sod off.'

He glared at Bertie. 'Well?'

Bertie pointed at himself, confused.

Dora softened. 'I don't think it's his fault, love. Think of all his suffering, here all on his own. No wonder he's a bit puddled.'

Bertie gave her a broad smile and nodded.

Horace threw up his arms. 'Suffering? Chuffing suffering, him? He doesn't know the meaning of the word ... or any others, come to that. It's my mother who's been suffering. Poor soul, thinking him dead all these past chuffing years. Dead, a war hero. My mother polishing his bloody Victoria Cross, won posthumously for storming a German machine-gun nest single-handed. Only nests he's ever stormed are the birds in this wood.'

He paced, snarling. 'Shot in France, they told her. Twenty-five years, I ask yeh.'

Bertie's eyes flashed. He stirred the pot violently, muttering, 'Jerry Germans. Bertie kill them all. Not like Jerry Germans. I kill!'

Horace shouted, 'Kill? Thee kill? Tha wouldn't know a Jerry if he was stood in front of thee. And as for thee being in France, well, all I can say is tha ought to have been.'

Dora shrugged. 'But he got the VC, love.'

Horace shook his head. 'How he managed that ... well, I'll never know.'

Chapter 11

WANTED DEAD OR ALIVE

Behind tall gates, three metres high, and with walls to match, stood the hospital for the insane.

In its main office, the resident doctor sat answering his telephone. He wore a white smock and a medical cap. Though speaking in English, his words carried a heavy German accent.

The doctor sighed. 'Not so much a good day, Commander. What news of the lorry, our documents? Tomorrow, you say? I do hope so, Commander. I do hope.'

He replaced the phone in its cradle, then took a long drink from a bottle of schnapps. Slamming it down, he shouted in anger:

'English idiots! I vil shoot the three imbeciles!'

Chapter 12

THE GATHERING OF HUNTERS

It was late afternoon in Boggleswick and a large crowd had gathered outside the village post office. They were there to hear Police Constable Ginger Perkins speak on the traitorous action committed against the army by Horace.

A large poster had been pinned to the village notice board. It was a wanted poster asking if anyone had seen Horace. It read: *Have you seen this man?* Beneath the heading was a photograph of Horace, looking about thirteen years old, in school uniform. The poster went on to say he was a traitor and kidnapper, armed and dangerous, and that any sightings should be reported to the police or to a member of the military forces.

Mavis Miller, Bobby's sister, moved forward for a closer look. She shook her head and tutted. 'Who'd have thought it? Horace, son of a war hero. Old Albert, he'd turn in his grave if he knew.'

Babs Seymore spat. 'Kidnapped my Dora, he did. Took her from her warm bed. Wish she'd never bloody married him, I do. Our Jack's going crackers.' She dabbed her tears with a hanky.

Ginger raised a fist. 'He'll not dare show his face around here. My bet, he's off on one of them submarines, drinking schnapps wi' his German buddies. Wish I could get me hands on them.' He looked at tearful Babs and shook his head. 'Sorry, Babs, but if you ask me, well, sardines lie side by side in the same tin.'

Babs glared. 'Let me tell thee this, bloody PC Ginger Nut. If tha dares to put thee hands on my lass, I'll cut thee bollocks off and stick 'em in a chuffing sardine tin. Does tha hear me?'

She turned to the crowd. 'That goes for anybody else thinking of hurting my Dora.'

A voice rang out. Thelma Ritson stepped forward. 'Dora's nowt to do with this. She's my mate. She'd never dream of nicking owt, not even a cup of tea from t'canteen.'

Babs nodded her thanks.

Ginger shrugged. 'Err... well. We have men from His Majesty's army arriving tonight, and along with Captain Peter Strong and myself we'll work out a plan. I'll also put a call into Police Headquarters and ask for assistance.' He coughed. 'Babs, no harm will come to Dora. You have my word.'

Alfie Tucker, local hero known as Tupp of the Track raised his hand. He was an ex-boxer, runner, rugby player, do-gooder and charity worker, helper to all, but with a record of things always going wrong. Never married, still living with his mother, he announced, 'I can take some men, get them into shape. Fit as tigers they'll be.'

Ginger cut him off. 'Yes, but no thank you, Alf. I think we've more than enough help. We do appreciate the offer, but after the annual fishing holiday in Whitby, well, we must decline. Did finish up sinking the boat. Lucky for us there were no non-swimmers amongst us. May I suggest you join Jack Seymore and the home guard?'

He checked his watch. 'That'll be all for now. We meet here tomorrow morning. Keep your eyes and ears open.'

*

Meanwhile in the cave, Dora and Horace sat with army cutlery and tin plates while Bertie busied himself over a pot of stew.

Dora grimaced, nodding towards him. 'Please don't ask me to eat yeh dad's stew, Horace. I'm sick just watching him. When I asked what's in it, he just said "yum yum."'

Bertie heard the words and grinned. 'Yum yum, soon quarter past two.'

Horace sighed. 'I've got to agree with yeh, love. But I daren't upset him. If we push him too far, he'll chuck us out – and he could. Living like this for twenty-five years, no wonder his mind's gone.'

Bertie licked his spoon. Dora recoiled. 'Just look at his hands, Horace. How can anybody cook with hands like that?'

Bertie was wearing fingerless gloves, but his fingers were far dirtier than the gloves. He wriggled them and smiled.

Horace sniffed. 'He's got a strange earthy smell about him.'

Bertie sniffed himself. Dora sniffed the air too. 'Aye. Like summat gone off.'

Horace sniffed the stew, then sniffed Bertie. 'Summat's not right. He smells better than the pot.'

Bertie sniffed both, then dashed to a cupboard and pulled out a perfume bottle. He sprayed himself liberally, then held it up for them to see. The label read *Evening in Paris*.

Horace sniffed again and shook his head. 'That's definitely not an Evening in Paris. More like a night in the Black Hole of Calcutta.'

Dora frowned. 'It's muck, that's what it is. Your dad needs a bath. Even the kettle's cleaner than him. It's not that I can't cook – or won't. It's just I wish your mum were here. Even her burnt sausages.'

Horace sighed. 'You're right there, love. Pity. And I don't think he took the giblets out of that crow he put in. Come to think, did he pluck it?'

They glanced at Bertie, who dipped his fingers into the stew, licked them and beamed. 'Yum yum soon.'

Horace turned to the army food supplies and pulled out two tins. 'Looks like we're dining courtesy of His Majesty's army, love. I'm not ready to become a bloody werewolf yet.'

Dora shivered. 'Werewolf? You don't think your dad... you don't think he's the Wolf Man of Bogie Wood?'

Horace hugged her. 'Could well be. All them stories our parents told us: if we misbehaved, the Wolf Man would get us. Could be him. But me dad's harmless, and he hasn't howled at us yet, has he?'

Bertie stopped stirring, pointed at himself and grinned. 'Me good cook. Bertie cook for Bertie's English friends. Yum yum, ready now.'

Horace shook his head. 'Sorry, Dad. But me and Dora, we're army rations. We eat sausage and mash, Yorkshire pudding. We're not used to your methods. Maybe Bela Lugosi, Lon Chaney and Boris bloody Karloff would enjoy it, but not us.'

Bertie rubbed his belly, eyes shining. 'All for Bertie. Make Bertie big and strong.'

Chapter 13

VILLAGE INN, THE RED LION

Sugar Brookes was tending bar at the Red Lion. Around the tables sat the regulars: men too old for the forces. Helping behind the counter was his vivacious barmaid, blonde bombshell Suzy Bond.

Nearest the bar sat the local blind beggar, Tapper Tomkins, with dark glasses and white cane. Jockey Scobie, Forweather Tony Cantaloni and Syles Stiff were all talking anxiously about the latest news – Horace, the lorry, the search.

Sugar shrugged and turned to Suzy. 'Well, he's certainly stirred some shit, has young Horace. Given them summat else to talk about. Not heard a word about racing, football, cricket.' He glanced at Suzy's open blouse. 'Not a mention of your tits. And believe me, that's got to be something good to stop them nattering and gaping at them beauties.'

Suzy winked. 'There's not the only eyes been giving them the once-over. Seen thee frothing at the mouth n'all. Tha can count thee self as one.'

The inn fell silent as the door opened. Father O'Conner entered. Walking over, he signalled to Sugar.

'Be a shot of the usual, Father?' Sugar asked.

The priest smiled. 'You know my poison, Sugar my boy. Top it to a double Irish.' He winked at Suzy, his eyes twinkling at the blouse, then winked again at Sugar.

'Err, has someone dropped that five-pound note over there?' He pointed to the corner, near Tapper's seat.

Like a flash, Tapper lifted his dark glasses and scanned the floor. The room roared with laughter.

Father O'Conner winked. 'See, we're still at it, Tapper?'

Tapper lowered his glasses. 'Who's that? Is that you, Father?'

Scobie laughed. 'Tha can't kid a kidder, Tapper. Father's got thee well weighed up. That right, Father?'

O'Conner smiled. 'That's for sure, Scobie. Old Taps has been at that game too long. Doesn't know everyone's wise to him now. Sorry about the racing, Scobie. Same story for Billy Preston's lad. Signed for the Villa, now he's shooting them in France. Hope he makes it home in one piece. Fine player, that lad.'

Seeing Scobie's face fall, the priest gave him a pat on the shoulder.

Scobie sighed. 'Aye, it's a bit of a struggle. But nothing compared to what our lads are going through in France. True, I've nowt coming in with sport cancelled, but we'll get by. We always do.'

Sugar butted in. 'Tell thee what, Scobie. Why don't that borrow a pair of dark glasses and join Tapper? Or better still, join the home guard. Least tha'll get thee grub.'

The priest held up his hand and removed his cap. Circling the inn, he motioned for donations. At Tapper's table he dipped into the tobacco tin and plucked out a shilling.

Tapper raised his glasses but said nothing.

The Father moved on to Scobie, holding out his cap. Scobie reached, smiling. 'Thanks, Father. It'll certainly help me out.'

O'Conner slowly shook his head. 'Oh no, Scobie. Hard times we're in, with a war on. You wouldn't be thinking of taking money from our Lord, now?'

Ashamed, Scobie muttered, 'Noooo, Father. Misunderstood, I did.'

'I thought so,' O'Conner replied smoothly. 'Scobie Forweather, taking money from the church? Never. He'd sooner make a small donation. Ten bob, shall we say?'

He glanced at Tony and Syles, who each added a ten-bob note to his cap. Pocketing the money, the priest set his hat back on and made for the door.

'Err, just a second, Father,' Sugar called after him. 'Ain't we forgetting something? Payment – double Irish?'

He winked.

The priest snarled, tossed a few coins on the bar and exited the inn.

Chapter 14
VILLAGE HALL OFFICE

Jack Seymore was sitting at a desk reading a comic when Sammy Simpson entered. Both wore home guard uniforms. Sammy's uniform was far too large, the belt holding his trousers up under his armpits.

Sammy was furious. 'Now look here, Seymore, can tha do owt about these uniforms? Lads are not happy bunnies, I can tell thee.'

Jack stood and inspected Sammy's outfit. Sammy eyed Jack's uniform, which fitted him perfectly.

'See, tha's got a good un.'

Jack ran his hands down his well-fitted tunic. 'Aye, I'm rather pleased wi' my good fortune. It being the only one wi' stripes.'

Sammy pointed to his own sleeves, where the stitching showed stripes had once been. 'Good fortune, my arse. They were delivered to your house.'

Jack shrugged. 'Aye, that's right. I had Babs take it up to fit. Tha should do same, Sam.'

Sammy laughed. 'Then I'd need a bloody wife. I don't buy trouble.'

Jack hurried to change the subject. 'Has lads all gone home, then?'

Sammy nodded, still angry. 'They've just gone. Juddy Forweather's trouser bottoms are just below his chuffing knees, an' wi' his jacket cuffs up to his elbows he's right down in't dumps. He wanted to go into Flamdale wi' his new girlfriend, show her his uniform.'

Jack butted in. 'Can't tha swap him for thine?'

Sammy laughed. 'Tha can't be serious. He's already got the biggest uniform there was. He's six-foot-eight. Can't find boots to fit him. Can't believe little Scobie's the lad's father.'

Jack nodded and spread his arms. 'I'll ask Captain Strong to see what he can do. In't morning tha can tell Juddy. I'm not promising, mind. He's already on about getting us rifles. Headquarters reckon we need specialist training, and they've not got the men at the moment.'

Sammy snorted. 'That reminds me. Lads don't want to be marching about wi' bloody broomsticks on their shoulders. Everybody's laughing at 'em. Hitler'd invade tomorrow if he knew.'

Jack scratched his brow. 'I tell thee, it's only temporary—'

The phone rang. Jack picked it up. 'Home Guard Sergeant Seymore. Yes, Sir. I'll see to it, Sir. In morning, you say? What about billeting? Oh, I see. Good day, Sir.'

Sammy leaned forward, curious. 'Who was that, Jack?'

Jack shrugged. 'That was Captain Strong, Sammy.'

'What's that bureaucrat want?'

Jack rolled his eyes. 'That man just happens to be your employer, Sam. You've worked as his gamekeeper six years to my knowledge. You should know him better than me. Peter's not a bad chap.'

Sammy narrowed his eyes and gave a sly smile. 'Oh, it's "Peter" now, is it? Tha didn't call him Peter when tha were at his pheasants, thee and that mate o' thine, Stiff. I think I heard thee call him something else. Remember, Jack? I kept me mouth shut. Didn't report yeh both.'

Jack stamped his foot. 'Now that were a long time ago, Sammy. Tha's got to learn to forgive and forget.'

Sammy jabbed a finger at him. 'Aye, it's "learn to forget" since tha's been eating his salmon and his game. Don't think village don't know about Babs and her little trips up t'estate.'

Jack's face turned white. He was stunned at what Sammy had said.

'Well, I'll be off then, Jack. Back to some corned beef and hash. Eh, Jack?'

Jack wasn't listening. He was in another world, staring into space as the door shut behind Sammy.

Jack shouted in rage. 'I'll bloody swing for her! I'll give her salmon and game, I'll give her chuffing presents, I'll give her two black eyes! Oh, you've got it coming, girl, you've got it coming!'

Suddenly there was a bang at the window. Jack nearly jumped out of his skin. Sammy's face grinned through the glass.

'Bloody hell, Sam. Tha near frightened me to death!'

Sammy shouted, 'Tell Babs to save me a bit of that duck. Forgot what it tastes like!'

Jack hurled his comic at the window. 'Arrrrrh! Arrrrrh!'

Chapter 15
BATH NIGHT

It was a rainy night in Bogie Wood. Horace stood over a makeshift bath he had fashioned from the lorry's canvas. Dora poured water into it from a red fire bucket. She smiled. 'Nearly full, Horace love. Where's your dad?'

Horace looked around anxiously. 'Think he's scarpered, love. Crafty old bugger worked out what we were doing and shot off like a rat up a drainpipe.'

Dora raised a finger. 'Do you think it might be that I'm here, Horace? Me being a woman?'

Horace nodded. 'Could have a point there, love.'

Dora sighed. 'I remember Gippy Brown telling us at school how his dad used to put all of them in a boat in their back yard. You remember Gippy, Horace? There were six of 'em. He had five sisters. He'd chuck in the soap and tell them all to scrub like mad. Then he'd throw in hundreds of buckets of cold water.'

Horace frowned. 'Why didn't he fill the boat first?'

'Full of holes, that's why. One of his sisters, Ethel, told me they used to get splinters in their bums.'

Horace checked his watch. 'Where's that chuffing idiot gone?'

Dora dipped her hand in the water. 'He may like a warm

bath, Horace. This is cold. We could put a few hot kettles in for him.'

Horace laughed, holding up Bertie's tiny kettle. 'Wi' this? We'd be lucky to get two cups out of it.' He cut a large piece of canvas with a bayonet.

Dora scratched her head. 'Are we having two baths, Horace? One for us?'

He shook his head. 'No love. It's just a screen. Give him a bit of privacy. Might just do the trick.'

From behind the stacked supplies came a noise.

Dora clutched Horace. 'Owwwwooo, Horace, what's that noise? Not rats, is it?'

Horace hugged her. 'No, silly. No rats in here. If there had been, Bertie would've had them in his pot.'

Bertie crept out of the shadows, staring at the bath in horror. 'Bertie don't want wash. Bertie clean.'

Horace waved him forward. 'Come into light. Let's have a butchers at thee.'

Dora pointed. 'What's in his hands, Horace?'

Bertie rushed forward and opened his hands. Out jumped a frog. Dora screamed. Bertie picked it up and dropped it in the bath, grinning. 'Bertie clean. Bertie wash.'

Horace and Dora rigged up the canvas screen with clothes props.

'He's been in the river, he has,' Horace muttered.

Dora pinched her nose. 'Think he's been in more than the river. He stinks.'

Together, they grabbed the unsuspecting Bertie and threw him, clothes and all, into the bath. Horace leaned close to his ear. 'Bertie not clean. Bertie stinky. But Bertie gonna be clean. Bath for Bertie boy.'

Shivering, Bertie sat in the water. Horace scrubbed at him with a block of army-issue carbolic soap. The bathwater turned black, weeds and insects floating on top.

'Sorry, Bertie, but them clothes have got to come off. Clothes too.' Horace stripped him down to his longjohns … and found underneath a pair of ladies' bloomers.

Bertie clutched them tight. Horace grinned. 'It's alright. Tha can keep thee bloomers on. We may find out what colour they are. Where tha got 'em from … well, I don't wanna know.'

Dora put a hand to her mouth. 'They look like your mum's, Horace.'

'What, black and stained?' Horace said.

'I didn't mean that! I meant your mum's, wi' elastic at the knees.'

Horace poked out his tongue. 'Oh, couldn't be the French frilly ones your mum wears?'

Bertie's head swivelled back and forth like a tennis spectator. Dora stood hands on hips. 'How do you know what my mum's knickers are like?'

Horace winked. 'Seen 'em on't line. All frilly.'

He went back to scrubbing his shivering father. 'Soon be over, Bertie.'

*

The following morning the whole village gathered at the post office. All heads turned at the sight of RSM Kennedy marching Eric, Percy and Bobby into the square.

'Left, left, left-right-left… shoulders back, Miller!' Kennedy bawled.

He brought them to a halt before Captain Strong, resplendent in a Hussar uniform. Snapping a salute, he reported: 'RSM Kennedy reporting for duty, Sir! Squad, stand easy!'

Captain Strong raised a hand from the platform. 'I needn't tell you why we're here. But for those of you completely ruddy brain-dead, let me repeat: we are here to capture and imprison one Private Horace Bagley.' He jabbed a finger. 'I have been told, in no way must you try to tackle this dangerous man.

Bagley is wanted for treason. He will be caught, or shot – dead or alive – and brought to me, or to PC Perkins, or to any of our army personnel.'

The crowd fell silent.

Babs raged, shouting above them all. 'My baby's not involved! Keep your paws off my baby! You ain't seen a war till you've seen Babs Seymore on the warpath. Be warned! Babs gives only one chance!'

Ginger Perkins raised his hands. 'Hush, hush. Let's not get too upset. Let me give you some facts. A vehicle – a lorry full of army supplies, destined for our boys in France – has been taken. I cannot stress enough the seriousness of this act. And by one of our own, the son of a man awarded the Victoria Cross posthumously.'

Whispers spread through the crowd. Strong cut in. 'Yes, like the Constable says. We'll clear this mess soon enough. We have the King's Own Royal Regiment here this morning. Sergeant Major Kennedy and his men, along with myself, will be concentrating on Bogie Wood, on the edge of my estate.'

He added, 'Constable Perkins has called headquarters. They're sending us Chief Inspector Brian Rumble of Scotland Yard. Aye, that's how serious this is.'

He waved Jack Seymore forward. Jack wore a head bandage. He snarled into the crowd.

'Horace Bagley is my son-in-law, as you well know. Always a cocky bugger. Why my Dora took to him, I'll never chuffing know. But she did. Don't let that stop you catching him. A clown, aye, who's shamed my family. If I get my hands on the bastard, the man who threw a chamber pot at me, I'll wring his chuffing neck! I'll kill him! He won't be coming back alive!'

Ginger pulled Jack down. 'Shuuush, Jack. Tha'll give yourself a heart attack. Go have a brandy. Think of getting Dora back.'

Jack, close to tears, pushed through the crowd. Babs caught his sleeve. 'What was all that about? Made a fool of yourself, you did. You were happy when they married. Said it were a marriage made in heaven. Got that wrong, yeh soft pillock.'

Sammy Simpson ran up, panting. 'Just caught thee before tha scraped off. We're all going down t'woods wi' Ginger. He's sent me to ask if tha coming.'

Babs snarled. 'Course he's coming. He's gonna catch that cocky little twat, ain't tha, Jack?'

Jack nodded and followed Sammy, who winked at Babs. 'Did tha save us a leg off that duck, Babs?'

Babs shook her fist. 'What in the chuff are you on about, Simpson? Watch that poisonous tongue o' thine or I'll cut it off. Don't try causing trouble between me and Jack. Don't push thy luck, Sammy boy.'

Jack strode back to his men with new pride, Sammy struggling to keep up.

Kennedy addressed the crowd. 'We believe Bagley is still in the area, no more than five miles away. The army vehicle hasn't been sighted. Every road, crook and cranny is covered. Someone's hiding him, or he's in that wood.'

Jack shouted, 'My men and I will front from the south side, RSM Bagley may take one of us, but not all of us!'

Kennedy coughed. 'Good man, Seymore. But be careful. You're not armed. Your brooms'll be no match for a 303 or a Bren gun. I'll accompany you myself. If we hit trouble, we'll sort it. Of this I'm sure.'

Kennedy pulled Eric aside, whispering in his ear. 'Swan, you're in charge. Protect your men. Head into the wood. If you make contact, blow this.' He pressed a bright silver whistle into Eric's hand.

Chapter 16
BATTLE OF BOGIE WOOD

Meanwhile, deep in Bogie Wood, Horace and Bertie had dragged one of the lorry's cab seats to the cave entrance. They set it down while Dora looked on, uncertain.

Horace asked, 'So, where do you want us to put it, love?'

Dora put a finger to her chin and pointed. 'Over there's best, love. Put it in the sun.'

The two men followed her gaze. A shaft of sunlight streamed through the trees into a clear patch. Bertie nodded, smiling. 'Dora come brown, like seaside.'

Horace shook his head. 'Aye, and burnt to a bloody cinder if she falls asleep. You sure you want to sit there, love? Wouldn't it be better out of sight? You know how to fire that rifle now. Took half the morning to teach thee.'

Dora nodded nervously. 'Yes, but I don't want to kill anyone, Horace. I don't think I could do it. Oooow, I'm frightened. Can't I come with you?'

Horace glanced at Bertie, who was shaking his head. He shrugged. 'Well, is it alright for her to come wi' us? Isn't she better wi' us?'

Bertie shook his head harder. 'Not good.' He waved his arms, spinning. 'Jungle full of tigers, lions.'

Horace laughed. 'Is tha on t'right planet? We're in England. We don't have chuffing tigers.'

Bertie disappeared back into the cave. Dora frowned. 'Where's he gone now, Horace?'

Horace looked skyward. 'God only knows. He ain't a full shilling. Tigers, lions… bet he's seen a few gorillas too.'

Bertie returned, smiling, something hidden behind his back. He pulled it out: the head of a tiger mounted on a plaque. The brass plate read: *Shot by Captain Peter Strong, 1937, Jaipur.*

Horace laughed. 'Aye, Father. A tiger shot in India. Silly old pillock.' He sighed at Dora. 'Wouldn't surprise me if there's owt left in the village after Dick Bertie Turpin's twenty-five years of plundering.'

Dora frowned. 'But I thought Dick Turpin was dead. He's not still alive, is he, love?'

Horace nodded towards Bertie. 'Very much alive, sweetheart. Very much alive. Come on, let's get on wi' Bertie boy's walk and trap inspection. I fancy a rabbit.'

*

At the same time, Kennedy and the home guard were moving in from the south side of Bogie Wood. Kennedy led the men of Boggleswick's home guard across a field at the edge. Jack and Sammy trailed slightly behind.

Sammy muttered, 'I tell thee, Jack, us lads going on this job wi' broomsticks is a load of bollocks, an' tha knows it.'

Jack shook his head. 'Horace chuffin' Bagley's only one man. Tha keeps forgetting. We are many. He hasn't a cat in hell's chance.'

*

On the western side, Eric, Percy, Bobby and Ginger were pushing into the trees.

Eric muttered to himself, 'Eric can smell thee, Bagley. Eric's coming for thee. Thee liver for me supper, Bagley. You traitorous git.'

Bobby whispered to Percy and Ginger, 'He's a psychopath. Lost it. He's not fit to lead us. Besides, he's only a private now.'

Eric stopped, spun around and grinned, sliding a round into the breech. 'I can smell him. He's near. Now get this: if anyone wants to leave, frightened wi' mumbo jumbo, Wolfman or no Wolfman, then piss off.' He thumped his chest. 'Nothin' in there. Nothin's gonna hurt Eric!' He screamed into the trees. 'You listening, Wolfman? Get back to your three little pigs. And you, Bagley.' Eric's eyes blazed. He shook all over. 'I know you're in there. Eric's takin' your heart out. Gonna fry it wi' your liver and onions. You hear me, Bagley?'

Ginger gasped. 'Steady on, Eric. No need for that silly talk.'

Eric turned on him. 'Look, mister carrot top, tha'd better step on it. And you two!' He glared at Percy and Bobby. 'Pair of idiots. Got me in this mess. Lost me my stripes by letting Bagley piss off wi' the lorry. Now move your legs! I'll shoot any traitorous pig that lags behind.'

Terrified, Percy and Bobby hurried after him.

*

Nearby, Horace and Bertie were setting a rabbit trap. Dora cocked her head. 'Shush. Listen, both of yeh.'

Horace nudged Bertie and pressed a finger to his lips. Bertie's eyes darted left to right. Shouting echoed through the trees.

Horace nodded. 'Yes, we've got visitors. Angry ones at that.'

Bertie cupped his ear. 'Kong... bear?' He clawed the air. 'Jerry German.'

Dora bit her nail. 'Ooooh, it's not Germans, is it, Horace?'

Bertie growled. 'I kill them all.'

Dora shivered. 'Let's go back to the cave, Horace. Bertie'll kill them all. Won't you, Bertie?'

Bertie bared his teeth, nodding.

Horace nodded too. 'Best get Dora safe. Bertie… I know that voice. It's that bastard Swanny. Bertie, wait here while I take Dora back. Don't take him on. Wait for me. Understand?'

Bertie shrugged. 'I kill him. He be very dead.'

'Do as I bloody ask thee. That's to chuffin' wait. Ok?'

Horace dragged Dora back towards the cave. Bertie sat casually on a log, lit a cigarette, coughed and stamped it out.

*

Eric pushed on, bellowing. 'Rigby! Miller! Carrot top! Where are you, trembling bags of shite?'

Percy and Bobby stumbled out of the undergrowth, Ginger gone.

'We're right behind thee, Eric,' Percy said weakly.

Bobby asked, 'Tha seen owt, Eric? Think he's in here?'

Eric snarled. 'No. But I can smell him. The little traitor's close.' He slid another round into his rifle. 'Dinner's main course. Bagley steak and liver. With meatballs. Mmm, nice.'

*

Bertie leapt up as Horace returned.

'Owt happened, Father?' Horace asked. 'Dora's worried. Swan's close, Bertie. He'll shoot me if he can.'

Bertie pointed to the clearing. 'Kong. He come very near. Growling.'

Horace sighed. 'What's tha mean, Kong? Told thee, no chuffin' gorillas in this country.'

Bertie threw back his head and howled like a wolf, screeched like a chimp and trumpeted like an elephant.

The sounds echoed through the trees. Percy and Bobby froze.

Bobby stammered, 'Yeh sure this is Bogie Wood, Percy? Are tha frightened? Cos I don't mind telling thee I am.'

Percy shook. 'Sounds like chuffin' Africa in there. I'm not a brave man, Bobby. Say the word and I'm out.'

Another almighty roar. Bobby clutched his backside. 'Percy, I'm off. I think I've shit mesen!'

Eric charged towards the sounds, grinning, lips wet. His boot hit a rope loop under leaves. The ground gave way, the rope snapped tight, and he was hoisted upside down.

'Aaaargh!'

Percy and Bobby bolted, holding their britches. Ahead, Ginger ran, crashing through undergrowth.

Eric swung like a pendulum, head five feet off the ground, firing wildly.

Bobby and Percy, panicked by gunfire, ran straight into a pit … and into a wild pig.

'Shoo! Shoo! Go on!' Bobby cried as the pig grunted and chased them round the pit.

Ginger, glancing back, sprinted into a bed of quicksand. He sank to his neck, flailing. A nailed sign read: *Gents Please Wash Your Hands*.

'Help! I'm in't God, it's bloody shit! I'm in shit! Help meee!'

*

On the wood's edge, the gunfire and screams froze the home guard. Sammy spat. 'Yeh can all bollocks to this. If tha thinks I'm walking in there wi' broomsticks, tha's mad. No way.'

The men turned and fled. Kennedy howled after them. 'Get back here! Cowardly dogs! Firing squads too good for you! This goes on my report!'

Jack shrugged. 'Err, I'll get 'em back, Sergeant Major. I'm as disappointed as you.'

Sammy snarled. 'Go on, kid thee sen, Jack. There's a war in there. I care about your daughter, but wi' broomsticks? Sorry, it's no go.'

*

Eric swung helplessly, rifle empty. 'Bagley! Come out an' fight me like a man, you coward!'

Horace and Bertie watched from bushes.

'Well, if it ain't Swanny boy, hung up like a kipper,' Horace whispered.

'Bertie catch mad Kong,' Bertie grinned.

Eric screamed. 'Miller! Perkins! Rigby! Cut me down, you cowards! Bagley, once I'm free, you die!'

Horace cupped his hands. 'Oh, I hear you, Swanny. Loud and clear.'

Bertie rushed from cover, grabbed Eric's chest with the rifle and pulled the trigger. *Click*. Empty. He smashed the rifle to the ground and stamped it flat.

Eric stared into Bertie's cross-eyed, broken-toothed grin. 'Woooooolf man…' he whimpered before fainting.

*

Later, Bobby, Percy and the pig huddled together in the pit, exhausted.

Horace stood over Eric, now cut down but catatonic. Bertie poked him with a stick. 'Him Jerry? He dead?'

Horace shook his head. 'He'll live. But not if we leave him. Got to get him where he'll be found. Whitby Road.'

Bertie started stripping Eric.

'Not yet, Bertie! He'll die o' exposure if tha keeps that up.'

Bertie redressed him in Bertie's rags, then twirled in Eric's uniform. 'Bertie soldier now. He Swanny enemy. We take to road. Very far. He heavy.'

Horace sighed and heaved Eric onto his back, struggling with the dead weight. Bertie marched ahead in Eric's uniform, rifle slung over his shoulder.

'This the easy way to Whitby Road?' Horace gasped.

'Bertie know. Big road, little bridge, mushroom field.'

Horace nodded. 'Aye. That's it. Get me there, Bertie. But we mustn't be seen. Invisible, that's us.'

An hour later, on the edge of Bogie Wood, Eric was tied securely to a tree where no one could miss him. He wore Bertie's old clothes: a blue ladies' coat with brooch, pit boots and odd football socks.

Chapter 17
A MOST SECRETIVE HOARD

Horace came rushing into the cave, exhausted and worried as he checked behind him. Dora was hiding nervously behind some of the lorry's crates.

'Halt! Who goes there, friend or foe?' she cried.

Horace jumped. 'Not Jesse chuffin' James. It's me, Dora. You scared me half to death!'

Dora stepped out of the alcove, hurt by his remark. Horace went to comfort her. 'Sorry, baby. I'm on edge. That silly chuff back yet?'

Dora turned her back. 'If you're referring to your wonderful father, then no. And what I said is what guards say.'

Horace sighed, kissed her neck and span her around. 'You're right, love. I should have known better. But I've been out ages trying to find me way back here. The silly old bugger left me to fend for myself.'

'Well, where is he? Where's dinner? I've heard you shooting all them poor little animals.'

Horace raised a finger. There was movement at the entrance. Dora clung to him as a figure stepped into the cave.

It was Bertie, now wearing a full-length leather coat, broad-shouldered with a high collar. On his head sat a Homburg, and in his hand a briefcase. He twirled like a model on parade.

Horace snapped. 'Where the chuff have you been? Leaving me to find my own way back? I could kill thee, I would – pissing off like that!'

Bertie spun until dizzy, then staggered into the armchair, holding up the case. 'Presents. Lorry under floor... lorry Bertie find.'

He handed over the briefcase. Horace carried it to a lamp, opened it and poured the contents onto the floor. Papers, maps and drawings spilled out. He squatted down.

'What have we here? Looks important. How? Where? Underneath lorry, tha says?'

Bertie nodded. 'Hidden. Bertie find hidden lorry.'

Dora wagged a finger at him. 'You'll go to prison, you will. You naughty boy.'

Bertie hung his head sadly.

Horace studied the papers. 'Dora, love, there's something queer here. Drawings of Armstrong's factory with maps. Markings on factories all over Yorkshire – Sheffield, Leeds, Hull. Dozens more. Dad's found something that wasn't meant to be found. Something meant to be shipped over to France.'

Dora's eyes widened. 'Secrets, Horace? Secret papers?'

Bertie perked up. 'Bertie dun good?'

Horace patted him. 'Aye, tha's dun good, Father. Only thing is, we can't understand these notes. Looks like German. And that's the problem. Who can we trust to translate without giving us up to the army or police?'

Dora thought hard. 'If only my friend Pru was here.'

Horace jumped. 'Pru? Your friend Pru Pringle, the schoolteacher?'

Dora nodded. 'Yes. Pru. She can speak French, Spanish and German. But she's at Cramers, a posh girls' school. Private. You have to pay to go there.'

Horace groaned. 'Just our luck. Posh schools, all down south. So we can count Pru out.'

Dora laughed. 'Don't be daft. Pru's not down south. She's only about a mile away, teaching at Trymore House. That big old place on Pastures Road.'

Horace paced. Bertie picked up a map, turned it upside down and scratched his beard.

Horace shook his head. 'One thing's for sure: Pru won't come here, fugitives or not. Bogie Wood? No one dares, not with tales of the Wolfman.'

Suddenly Bertie piped up. 'Bertie go to girls' school. Bertie get Poo.'

Horace chuckled, shrugged at Dora. 'Aye, we could send Bertie. I'm sure Pru would come with him. A handsome, athletic male, dressed like the man from an insurance company.' He turned to Bertie. 'Her name's Pru, not chuffin' Poo.'

Then Horace's eyes lit up. 'Wait a minute. Sorry, Dora, but… aye, that's it. We've got to kidnap Pru.'

Bertie rubbed his hands together. Dora glared daggers.

'Have you lost your marbles? Kidnap my friend? You'll stir up the army, the police, everybody. It's a bad idea, Horace. Think of something else. Please.'

Horace shook his head. 'We've no choice, sweetheart. It's our only chance to survive and get out of the mess I've got us in.'

Dora picked up some notes and frowned. 'Can't make head nor tail of these.'

Horace snatched them. 'That's because they're written in German. Bosch writing, this.'

'Never heard of him,' Dora muttered. 'Who's Bosch?'

Horace threw up his arms. 'Bosch means German, you daft bugger!'

Dora wandered to the transmitter, flicked a switch and turned the dial. Whistles, then foreign voices, then music.

*

Dora sat listening to orchestral music, cup of tea in hand. Horace pored over the papers. Bertie snored in a tin bath.

Horace muttered, 'These maps. Hull docks circled. Sheffield steelworks circled. Bloody targets. And this stamp – Luftwaffe. That's the German Air Force.'

He picked up Bertie's leather coat, checking the label: *Hergestellt in Hamburg.* In the pocket he found a black packet of cigarettes, a silver swastika embossed on it.

He lifted the Homburg. Inside: *Vostrich Berlin.*

Kicking the tin bath, he woke Bertie. 'Are you sure these clothes were in that lorry?'

Bertie shook his head. 'Case in lorry. Coat, hat in barn. Estate.'

Horace rubbed his chin. 'Aye. And I bet that's not all that's in yon barn. You know what this means?'

Bertie nodded, then shook his head. Dora frowned, then shook hers too.

'It means we've got spies.'

Bertie's eyes lit up. 'Mince spies? Christmas? Santa?'

Horace pointed at the transmitter. 'Hear that? Foreign voices. Germans. And these,' he said, holding up the cigarettes, 'German bloody fags. The Jerries are here. Not soldiers. Spies. The soldiers'll come later.'

Chapter 18
THE ASYLUM

Eric had been brought into reception at the Flamdale Asylum Medical Centre for the Insane. He'd been found tied at the side of the Whitby Road by two passing motorists, his state and dress prompting them to bring him in.

But Eric wasn't without company. Sitting on benches in a long corridor were Percy, Bobby and Ginger. Bobby held onto a lead with the pig attached.

Eric sat strapped to a dentist-type chair, still dressed in Bertie's cast-offs. A single overhead lamp shone down on his head. Fixed to it was an electrode cap that held him rigid. His eyes darted nervously about the room, his lips quivering. He strained at the shackles, but they held firm.

Outside, his three comrades had been rescued and were undergoing medical checks. Percy and Bobby sat together on a long bench, scarves tied across their mouths and noses. Their uniforms were filthy and torn. Ginger sat at the far end, stinking vilely, his uniform caked in dried excrement. Wearing a gas mask, he tugged and fidgeted, fighting his own stench.

Suddenly, screams and yells burst from the treatment room.

The three looked at each other in alarm. Eric's voice echoed down the corridor:

'Baaagleeeee! Take this bloody contraption off me! You hear meeee? You wolf-loving son of Satanism! I'll bite yeh bleeding head off! Eric's coming for yeh! I'm on my way, boy! Ha ha ha ha! Bagleeeee!'

Ginger, sitting nearest the treatment room door, shuffled quickly down the bench, edging closer to Percy and Bobby. Through the mask's faceplate, his eyes showed pure terror.

Percy jabbed a finger at him and snarled, 'Tha can get thee sen back up there! Tha's not sitting near us wi' that shit on thee!'

Inside, Eric stamped his feet in a frenzy, snarling and frothing at the mouth. He froze, listening to the muffled voices outside. It was only Percy, Bobby and Ginger, but the raving Eric didn't know that.

He bellowed: 'I can hear you, Bagleeeee, yeh bastard! Eric knows yeh there, you low-lying skunk! I can smell yeh! Oh, I'm coming, Bagleeeee! You're a dead man! A dead man, you hear meee! Ha ha ha ha!'

The lunatic screams, laughter and violent banging rang through the corridor. Percy, Bobby and Ginger toppled over each other in a desperate dash for the exit.

Chapter 19
TEA AT MAY'S

Night had fallen and all activities had been suspended after the incidents in Bogie Wood.

Horace asked Bertie, 'That transmitter radio set thing – that come from the barn?'

Bertie nodded. 'Bertie find in barn, hidden under hay.'

Horace went over and ruffled Bertie's hair. Bertie immediately took out a near-toothless comb and smoothed the spot. Horace sniffed his hand, pulled a face, then walked over to a rickety old rocking chair. He sat, hands behind his head, rocking in time to the orchestral music still coming from the transmitter: a piece from *Carmen*.

The chair suddenly collapsed, tipping Horace sideways to the floor.

'What the—!' he yelped.

Bertie grinned. Dora swallowed back her laugh, hiding it behind her hands. Horace struggled up, then kicked the chair in irritation.

'I've got it!' he cried.

Dora and Bertie both looked at him. Dora shrugged and sniggered. 'Got what, love? Back pain?'

Horace, eyes bright: 'Pru. Prudence Pringle. Your mate, Dora love. We can do this!'

Dora frowned. 'Do what, love?'

'Get Pru here. It'll work! Only way. That's if she's still living on Firbeck Street. Is she, Dora?'

Dora shrugged. 'She's never married, that I do know. Lives with her mum. Yes, she's still there. I see her going to work on her bike sometimes.'

Bertie dashed over to the wall where the postman's bike leaned. He pointed. 'Bertie's bike! Bertie got bike!'

Horace gave him a look. 'Bertie got bike? Yeh, nicked. That's Jake Wootton's, our postman. That's his chuffing bike. Post Office won't give him another, poor bugger. And yeh wonder why the pissing mail's always late.'

Horace rushed to Dora, pulled her into his arms and whirled her around before kissing her. Then he gave Bertie a wink. Bertie quickly ducked behind an old armchair, using it as a shield from the amorous Horace.

Horace stopped, a bit dizzy, then did a quick jig. Dora, bewildered, looked to Bertie, then mimed screwing a screwdriver into her brain. Bertie nodded solemnly, went to an apple box, pulled out an actual old screwdriver and handed it to her. Dora giggled.

She whispered to Horace, 'He makes me laugh, your dad, love. He's so funny.'

*

In the Bagley cottage front room, May poured tea for Thelma Ritson, Ethel Forweather and Angelina Cantoloni. Thelma had brought scones, Ethel jam tarts, Angelina cream.

May smiled. 'Nice to have a bit of company. I hope you don't mind, but I've asked Mirtle Swan round?'

The room fell silent.

'I know what yeh all must be thinking. But it's not her fault

Eric's a nutter. Met her in the post office, she said she'd think about it. She seemed upset by it all. Don't think she'll come, though.'

Ethel tutted. 'Tha must have a heart of gold, May. After what that man of hers said about what he'd do to your Horace.'

Angelina nodded, her Italian accent lilting. 'Let us not talk about. Let us enjoy.' She spooned cream onto a cut scone and handed it to May. 'Enjoy.'

Thelma smiled. 'Yes, Angelina's right. Let's enjoy ourselves with this lovely tea. We all know there's got to be a reason for Horace acting like he did. Horace ain't that bad a man.'

May sighed deeply. 'Thanks. It's nice to know I've got a few friends left. If you must know all the talk … well, I don't believe a word of it. Mavis Miller told me her brother Bobby says Eric Swan's not a full shilling. He's locked up in Flamdale Asylum, gone completely mad. Shouting out "Wolf Man!" and Horace's name, calling Horace the devil's child. Now I know he's crackers.'

They all nodded in agreement.

Ethel added, 'It'll all come out in the end, just you wait and see. That Babs Seymore, saying Dora should never have married Horace. Well, she's no sparkler, knowing what I know.'

All ears turned to her. May nodded eagerly. 'Yes, I've known for some time about her goings-on. I'm thinking it could be that Simpson for one, and her trips up to Lord Enfield's for another.'

May laughed, Thelma rubbing her hands in excitement. 'Come on, May, don't leave us in suspense. Tha can't stop now. Let's be knowing.'

May whispered: 'When Jack's away, then Babs goes out to play. Her little playmates are Simpson and the old lord of the manor.'

Thelma's eyes widened. 'No, I don't believe it. Does tha mean he… old Enfield… is shagging her?'

May smiled. 'Well, he's certainly not giving her singing lessons. But what he's doing is making her chuffin' sing.'

They burst out laughing.

Ethel nodded. 'Aye, that's what I heard. She's red hot for it. Our Scobie told me. Everyone knows but Jack.'

Thelma added, 'What's with His Lordship, though? We all know he's a bit of an old dog – eighty-four years old in a bloody bath chair. Surely she's not shagging him?'

They all giggled.

May whispered, 'Whatever she's doing, she's eating well. And she's wearing jewels and clothes that once belonged to Lady Caroline. So what she's doing to earn them little presents? Well, I can only imagine. Slowly killing the poor old bugger.'

Thelma shook her head. 'What about the manager, Captain Peter? Do you think he knows?'

Ethel smiled. 'He knows. Just turns a blind eye, he does. Anything to please his dad. It's all for the inheritance, yeh know. With Peter it's money first, cash is king. Wish my Scobie was like him.'

May laughed. 'What, looking after his money? Or, like his Lordship, riding a winner?'

Angelina interrupted. 'My Tony's family are all, how you call, sexy mad. They from Roma. They sell all the fine ice creams. The best in Roma. His brothers have many mistresses, too many. My Tony...' She picked up a knife from the table and mimed a cutting motion between her legs. 'He have only one woman. Angelina makes sure, only one woman.'

They clapped and laughed.

Thelma, still puzzled, asked, 'What I cannot understand is Sammy Simpson. Babs always gave the impression she hated the man.'

Ethel nodded. 'True, but it's an act on her part, especially with Simpson being so close to husband Jack. Our Sammy's the supplier of her fine dining table. Which she pays him in sexual activity.'

Thelma sniffed. 'Then Babs Seymore is no more than a common call girl, with her acts of prostitution. The Boggleswick bike.'

May laughed. 'Aye, you could well say that. The bike. I like that. She's not Yorkshire, remember. She's a southerner. Met that silly bugger Jack on a miner's welfare trip to London. She comes out of Soho. Enough said.'

Chapter 20
BERTIE THE POSTMAN

I t was late evening. The woodland was almost silent after the earlier shootings and cries for help, broken only by the occasional hoot of an owl. All the village search parties had long since returned to the safety of their homes.

In Bertie's cave, Horace slipped a letter into an envelope, licked it and stuck it down. On the front he wrote: *19 Flowitt Street*. He handed it to Bertie, who was dressed in Eric's uniform with his face blackened. Bertie motioned for a stamp.

Horace shook his head. 'No stamp.'

Bertie rummaged in his pocket, pulled out a large T-bone steak and handed it to Horace before tucking the letter into his tunic. Horace raised the steak, ready to slap Bertie with it, then turned to Dora, shaking his head.

'Hope the both of you can get it into your squirrel brains. We're in a chuffing do-or-die situation here. We've got to get this action right.'

Dora began dusting Bertie down with a stick, sending clouds of muck into the air. They all coughed. Horace waved the steak to clear the dust. 'Is everything clear? Clearer than it is in here, anyway – chuffing hell, Dora!'

Through the haze, Horace saw Bertie nodding. Dora prodded him. 'And don't forget to say Dora sends her love, Horace. You've not forgotten to tell May to tell me mum I'm alright, have you?'

Horace winked. 'Now, would I forget that?' He turned to Bertie. 'Main thing is: once Mum gets over the shock of seeing thee for the first time in twenty-five years, walking in like a ghost back from the grave, you make sure she gives this to Pru Pringle. Do you understand?'

Bertie nodded, smiling. 'May, my girl. Me give her kiss, kiss.'

Horace grabbed him by the collar. 'Kiss, kiss? Don't be surprised if Mum gives thee fist, fist! And if after twenty-five years you've forgotten where we lived, it's number nineteen.' Horace took Dora's stick and scrawled a 1 and a 9 in the dust. 'One-nine. Nineteen. Got it?'

Bertie blinked, then ran to a box, pulled out a perfume bottle and sprayed it under his arms and beard. He choked as the mist went into his mouth. Dora leaned in, sniffed and coughed.

'Oooow, what a pong. Not Evening in Paris. Where's it from?'

Bertie grinned. 'Smelly from farmer's. Man wash sheep. Stop Bertie scratching. No itch.'

Horace wagged a finger at him. 'Sheep dip? In a bloody scent bottle? Don't thee dare try to spend the night at Mum's. Realise, man, her tanks must be chuffing full after all these years. But I want thee back here, dost tha understand? Back here tonight.'

Bertie nodded, gave a salute of sorts, and was gone.

Horace turned to Dora, who had a cheeky look. She put one leg on a rock, hitched up her skirt, hand on hip, and winked. 'Time we started our honeymoon. How do you want me, love?'

Horace grinned. 'How about we use Bertie's tin bath?'

Dora, serious now, picked up a rifle and pointed it at him. Horace, hands raised, backed into a corner. 'Now Dora, steady on. That could go off. Stop mucking about, love. You've got me. I'm yours.'

*

Two miles away, at the Flamdale Asylum, Eric was still strapped to the chair. He sweated profusely, eyes flickering, babbling to himself.

'Corporal Eric... Colonel... lorry my fault... no, no, not my stripes, my stripes! That bastard Bagleeee!' He shouted: 'Bagley! It was him! Oh, he's with him – the Wolf Man, son of Satan! Living together, both of them! Eric knows! Bogie Wood! Bagleeee, you're a dead man! You hear meeee?'

The door opened. A man in a white coat entered, speaking English with a strong German accent.

'Tut tut. Be quiet! You're keeping my patients awake with your ramblings. It is not good that you shout. I am very angry at this.'

He tied on a surgical mask, shone a torch into Eric's eyes, then peered at him through a magnifying glass. Eric sobbed at the sight of the huge lens.

'I am your good doctor, Dieter Klinsmann. And you are Eric... Eric Swan. Mmm. You have a terrible smell about you. Do you wish a bedpan?'

Eric whimpered and shook his head as much as the electrode cap allowed. Klinsmann patted his shoulder. 'There, there. Let it all out. Tell your good doctor and you'll feel better.'

He pulled a bag of sweets from his pocket, unwrapped one and popped it into Eric's mouth. 'A nice little humbug for you.'

Eric sucked ravenously, managing a faint smile. Klinsmann leaned close. 'See? The good doctor is kind, yes?'

Eric nodded, opening his mouth to show the sweet was gone.

'Ah, a chomp, eh? My humbugs do not last long with you, I see.' Klinsmann dangled the bag. 'I may give you them all... once you tell me what I want to know. We start with the army vehicle, yes? Where is it?'

Eric whispered, 'Bagley... Bagley... the Wolf Man... not Eric.'

'Louder, Eric.'

Eric screamed: 'Bagley! Bagley! The Wolf Man! They know, not Eric!'

Klinsmann's eyes narrowed. 'You leave me no choice. I am not your friend. And you do not want me as your enemy.'

He slammed a fist on the table, strode to the control box and pressed the red button. The meter needle quivered as the cap on Eric's head glowed. Eric shook violently, convulsing as the voltage surged.

Klinsmann shut it down, slapped Eric's cheeks and shone the torch in his eyes. Eric slumped, barely conscious.

Klinsmann went to the phone, dialled and drummed his fingers. 'Is that you? Swan. I don't think he knows. Shall I dispose of him? Yes, he's still alive. You're sure?… Very well. I'll try again tomorrow. Good night, Commander.' He hung up, shook his head at Eric and left.

*

Near midnight, in Boggleswick village square, the streets lay deserted. Bertie crouched behind the monument, clutching the letter. He muttered to himself: 'One-nine. One-nine.'

A door opened. Jack Seymore stepped out in long johns, cardigan and nightcap, unsteady on his feet, smoking.

From inside, Babs bellowed: 'Is tha gonna get thee sen back in here and shut that bloody door? It's chuffin' freezing, yeh daft pillock!'

Jack slurred back, 'Coming, my sweetheart, coming!' He flicked his cigarette away, slamming the door behind him. The number "16" on the house shifted as one screw gave way, leaving it to read "19."

Inside, Babs stood at the mirror in a frilly French nightgown, powdering her face. Jack poked his head in.

'Tha sitting up all night in the dark ain't gonna bring our Dora back. And wearing that bloody thing'll have thee catching thy death. Come to bed wi' thee old man, eh? I'll warm thee up.'

Babs smirked through the mirror. 'Warm me up? Tha couldn't warm me if tha chucked this fire on me. Piss off to bed. Tha's been on jungle juice again.'

Jack belched, slammed the door and trudged upstairs. Babs heard the bedsprings creak as he jumped in. She clapped her hands, lit a candle, waved it by the window, then blew it out and opened the sash a crack. She sprayed perfume over herself and the settee, then lounged, waiting.

Outside, Bertie saw the candle signal, checked the number – 19 – and shuffled to the window. He puffed on Jack's discarded fag, coughed, then climbed inside.

Babs whispered huskily, 'It's open, sweety pie. You brought baby doll something nice?'

Bertie stumbled forward, knocking a flowerpot.

'That'll cost thee, clumsy sod. Be quiet, or you'll have him up!'

Feeling his way, Bertie handed over trinkets from his pockets: a porcelain figure, then a perfume bottle.

Babs cooed, spraying perfume onto her cleavage. 'Oh, lover boy. Better than the trout and duck eggs last week. Come on, get thee nose down here and have a good snifter.'

Bertie grew frantic, confused, pawing and slobbering at her. 'More kiss, kiss. Bertie want more kiss, kiss!'

Suddenly Babs froze. She lit a match, held it up and screamed at the sight of the cross-eyed, hairy man grinning at her.

'Jack! Jack! Wolf Man! Wolf Man in our house!'

Bertie panicked, bolted through the window and landed in the flowerbed, bumping straight into Sammy Simpson, sneaking down the garden wall with a basket of game, wine and flowers. Bertie knocked him flat, then sprinted into the dark.

Sammy scrambled up, gasping, brushing dirt from his clothes. His flowers lay crushed on the path, his basket gone.

'Me basket... where is it? Why, the thieving little bastard!'

Chapter 21

INCIDENT AT ENFIELD MANOR

Three days later

Late at night in Lord Enfield Manor House, Captain Peter Strong was lying in bed reading. Lady Caroline sat at the dressing table combing her hair. She stopped, rose and made for the four-poster bed. She was wearing a pair of Peter's pyjamas. Getting in, she cuddled up and rubbed her body against the Captain's back.

Peter whispered in her ear. 'Are you cold, darling?'

Caroline sighed. 'A little, my love.'

Peter snarled in anger. 'Aye, the whole house! I'm afraid he's never had it warm, not since your ruddy logs were stolen. Someone's warming their arses on your logs. I'm ruddy sick of all this thieving. That Ginger Perkins… well, he couldn't catch a ruddy cold, what!'

Caroline wrapped her legs around him and hugged. 'Yes, my sweet, he never found the culprits that took the coal. He's a complete waste of time, if you ask me.' She kissed Peter's neck and they rolled about the bed from one side to the other. Peter smiled.

'But I've got you to keep me warm, my precious. A man could not ask for more.'

They rolled and rolled, Caroline panting like a dog on a hot day. They tumbled out of bed. Peter made to return, but Caroline held him back.

'Let's do it on the carpet, my sweet.'

Peter kissed her. 'But, my love, he will hear us. He's a very light sleeper, as you well know.'

Caroline, husky. 'Bollocks to him. Come to me, I'm on fire.'

Caroline knelt over Peter's chest, pulled off her pyjama top and tore at his, buttons popping everywhere. She moaned as she ripped off his long johns. Peter's eyes rolled.

'Steady on, gal, you'll be having a ruddy heart attack. Wearing those horrible Jim-jams, his Christmas present to me. Just think of it, my sweet. We're making love while he sleeps next door. You adulterated, you.'

She giggled. 'Don't you mean the ones he gave you that he'd worn out? The Scrooge of a man. But who cares? Who wants his money? I've got you, my love.'

She pawed his body and made cat-like sounds, purring. 'I'm a tiger, darling, and I'm coming to tear you apart.' She growled.

*

On the patio outside, Jack was creeping about. He looked up at the balcony and its French windows. Against the curtains he could see the silhouettes of a man and woman. They appeared to be hugging and kissing, the woman chasing the man about. Jack clenched his fists, eyes blazing, snarling.

'Caught you. If I hadn't seen it with my own eyes, I wouldn't have believed it. You and Peter. You... you scarlet woman. You bloody no-good adulterer.'

He heard cries and moans. He saw the doors were partly open. His face turned crimson, teeth grinding. Noticing a trellis of ivy up the wall, Jack began to climb. Reaching the balcony, he heard Caroline gasp huskily.

'Ohhh, Peter.'

Peter, in ecstasy: 'Oh, sugar plum. Ohhh, it's sheer bliss.'

Caroline: 'I know, I'm in heaven… oooowwweee.'

Peter: 'Me too, my sweet. I'm floating on a cloud, my petal.'

Caroline rubbed his chest. 'To think I've been sharing a bed with a drunk, sodden corpse all these years. Lying with a lifeless body, a dying man gasping for breath.'

Jack snarled, shaking his head. 'What the chuff's going on here? Bloody sleeping with a dying man… aye, it's not who, it's how pissing long. I must have been blind. Me working me bollocks off for that woman. I'm beginning to think if our Dora's mine. Jesus Christ.'

Inside, Caroline gasped: 'It's so good with you, my love. Like running through a meadow naked, the grass whipping my thighs, and you, my love, standing there like the statue of David amongst the poppies and butterflies. Your baton in your hand.'

Peter's face glowed with pride. 'Like David, you say? Do you really think so, petal? Then we must sail away into our sunset. You must leave that man. Say your goodbye.'

Caroline sighed. 'In time, my love, in time. We must be patient, my David.'

Jack climbed onto the balcony, silently pulled back the door and entered. From behind the curtain he surveyed the room. Seeing a gun in a display cabinet, he took it out. It was an old civil war weapon, already loaded. He pulled back the hammer. Caroline and Peter were rolling about on the carpet. Jack shouted.

'Come out, yeh adulteress bastard! I'll bloody well give thee grass on the thighs! Come out, chuffin' David, 'cause Goliath's come to see thee. Bloody Captain Peter Strong! Come out, yeh snake in the grass, you hear me?'

Peter and Caroline froze. Terrified, Peter tried to crawl under the bed. He hit his head on a chamber pot. Caroline whispered: 'Who is it? You've not been cheating on me, have you, Peter?'

Peter snarled. 'Sounds like that ruddy home guard arsehole Jack Seymore. What's he on with? Adulterer? I wouldn't touch that woman of his with a ruddy barge pole.'

Caroline peeked up and saw Jack pointing the gun. She ducked back down. 'He's got a gun, Peter. He's going to murder us both. I don't even know the man, so what's his game?'

Peter stammered. 'I don't understand.'

Caroline punched him. 'Well, get your brain thinking, man. Ask him. Go on!'

Jack's shouting woke Lord Enfield. From the next room came his tremulous voice: 'Caroline... what the hell's going on?'

Jack roared: 'Come out, yeh bastard. Steal a man's wife, would yeh? After all these lying, cheating years, only place she'll be going is joining you six feet under.'

The lord buried his head under the blankets. Peter knelt and peeked over the bed. Jack raised the gun. Peter ducked. Jack circled and fired at his backside, but the old gun backfired, puffing smoke into Jack's face and throwing him backwards.

Peter and Caroline seized their chance. Naked, they fled the room with only a sheet.

Lord Enfield's voice rang through the wall: 'Can anyone tell me what the hell's going on?'

Jack staggered up, grabbed a cutlass from the cabinet and chased Caroline, who screamed, running for her life down the stairs. Jack brandished the cutlass from the landing. Peter darted into the lord's bedroom, slamming and locking the door. Jack, torn, chose to chase Caroline.

Growling: 'Oh no, tha don't. Come here, yeh hussy. Not bloody good enough for yeh? Yeh got it wrong, darling. It's me who's too good for you, lady.'

Caroline screamed: 'I don't know you! I'm not your prostitute wife. Are you mad? Get out of my home. Leave me alone, you idiot. Has my Gerald sent you?'

Jack stopped. 'Gerald? Bloody Gerald? Another of your playthings? Who the chuff's Gerald?'

Caroline turned, defiant. 'Gerald, Lord Enfield. My husband, if you must know.'

Jack stared, trembling. He dropped the cutlass, clutched his head. 'I'm so very sorry, m'lady. I thought... I heard my wife Babs was here. She's been here. I've seen the presents. Oh, what have I done?'

Caroline sighed. 'What have you done? I'll tell you. You've stopped me making a terrible mistake. I thought Peter Strong loved me. When I needed protection, he ran and hid, leaving me to face you alone. Oh, we've both made mistakes. Let's think no more on what's happened tonight. Thank you, Jack.'

Chapter 22
PLAN B

Bertie was now sporting a black eye. He sat in the old armchair, holding a piece of salmon to it, which he nibbled on from time to time. Horace paced in front of him, arms behind his back. Dora was making sandwiches from the basket Bertie had delivered. Horace paced the cave, angry. He turned to Bertie.

'Let's start from the beginning, eh? Let's get this right—'

Dora interrupted him. 'He's brought us some lovely food, Horace love.'

Horace looked at her, holding up his hands. 'Excuse me, but I was saying... err... where was I? So I'm gathering that the chuffin' happy wanderer here,' he pointed at Bertie, 'gets into the village unseen. Am I right?'

Bertie nodded and grinned.

'Good, that's a bloody relief. Furthermore, that he found the house, number nineteen. One bloody nine. My mum's, May's. Am I right?'

Bertie nodded.

'Good. OK, you found the house.'

Bertie raised a finger, drew a "1" and "9" in the air and said: 'One nine, nineteen... come to mama, Canada man... in dark, kiss.'

Horace snapped round. 'That's what she said to thee, my mum? Chuffin' "kiss, kiss" – my mum?'

Bertie dug into his pocket and pulled out a framed photograph. He handed it to Horace, who looked at it. The picture showed Jack and Babs in Cleethorpes with a little girl sitting on a donkey.

'What the— Dora, you better look at this, love. Now I'm really confused.'

Dora looked up at Horace, who was offering her the photograph. She walked over, took it and put a hand to her mouth.

'Where did you get this, Bertie?'

Bertie looked at them both, his face saddened, like he'd done something wrong.

'Mama… mama's house. Number nineteen. Sexy mama.'

Dora shook her head. 'No, not number nineteen. Number sixteen. This came from my mum's front room. That's my mum and dad, with me at the seaside. See, it says Cleethorpes on it. That's me on Freddie the donkey. I'm only seven years old. That's when the picture was taken.' She looked to Horace. 'He's got the wrong house, Horace. He's been to my mum's. Oh, Horace… what's he done?'

Horace gave Bertie a stern look. 'That's not attacked Babs, has tha? Nah… couldn't have. Not with Babs. Yeh mum would've half killed him. And with your dad there, no way.'

Dora, worried, whispered to Horace: 'Horace… he could be one of them sex maniacs.'

Horace smiled. 'Now yeh gotta be joking. Bertie Cassanova Bagley? Don't make me laugh, love.'

Bertie looked hurt by the accusations hurled at him. He got up and walked out of the cave. Shouting back: 'Bertie not jump on mama. Mama jump on Bertie. Kiss! She sexy maniac, not Bertie!'

Horace hugged Dora and whispered in her ear. 'You know,

love… thinking about it, Bertie wouldn't attack your mum. There's got to be something else.'

Dora gave a smile. 'Yes, love, I think we may have really upset him. Let's tell him we're sorry. At least until we know the truth of it all.'

Horace sat in the armchair with Dora on his knee. He rubbed her back.

'Only trouble is, we haven't got that letter to Pru. We could have stirred the hornets' nest with last night's catastrophe. So it's Plan B now, I'm sorry to say. But it's our only chance remaining.'

Dora looked at him, questioning. 'Plan B? What's Plan B, love?'

Horace squeezed her tighter. 'Plan B is to…' He sighed. 'Kidnap Pru Pringle.'

Part Three

Chapter 23
DEAD OR ALIVE

Outside the Boggleswick post office, a worse-for-wear Captain Strong had gathered quite a crowd. He was pinning an artist's impression of Bertie to the notice board. The only likeness was Bertie's crossed eyes. The drawing showed him with large fangs and a full face of long hair.

"THE WOLF MAN. SHOOT TO KILL" was written underneath.

The crowd pushed forward, gasping at the horrendous drawing. The meeting was suddenly interrupted. A bus came down Main Street, pulling up beside them. The faces staring out of its windows were painted in a ghoulish manner: Count Dracula, Frankenstein's monster, vampires of every description.

The coach door opened and out stepped a man dressed in black, wearing a full-length cape, with bright red lipstick and false protruding teeth. He was imitating Dracula. Speaking in a Welsh accent, he smiled:

'We are on our way to visit the Master's grave. We be referring to Whitby Abbey? We seem to have lost our way. Could you be so kind... the right direction?'

Ginger, who had joined Captain Strong, sneered.

'Whitby? Master's grave? Well, let me give you the good news, Boy-O. Your "Master", as you call him, well, he's not dead. In fact, Boy-O, he's very much alive and bloody kicking, in yon wood.'

He turned Dracula towards Bogie Wood.

Dracula clapped his hands excitedly at the news, then rushed back onto the coach. Standing beside the driver, dressed in a plain blue jacket, he cried out to his passengers:

'He's here! Our Prince of Darkness is very near, my brothers and sisters. Can you not feel his presence?'

A man dressed as Baron Frankenstein stood with his companion, wrapped head-to-toe in bandages as the monster.

'Can't say I can see him. Who says he's near?'

The 'monster' nodded. 'Aye, where is he then? I hope it's not too far. Can't walk far wrapped up like this. These bloody pit boots are killing me.'

Dracula opened his arms wide and pointed towards the hillside and the great woodland known as Bogie Wood.

'He's there, my children. Living yonder, in the form of the Werewolf. He awaits our bidding. We must heed his call!'

He nudged the driver. 'See if you can't get the bus a bit nearer, Owen. As close as you can.'

Owen shrugged. 'Aye, but remember, I'm only the hired driver. I won't be joining in your adventure. It's only a bloody day trip, man. This bus leaves for Swansea at seven o'clock.'

Dracula and Owen looked at their watches together.

'Plenty of time. Half a day left. So forward, my son!'

The coach pulled away, heading towards the wood. Passengers waved at the crowd as they passed. Catholics crossed themselves. Local undertaker George Diggins rubbed his hands with glee.

Sugar grinned at him. 'Looks like tha'll be overflowing with work, George.'

George winked. 'Aye, Sugar lad. Always thought those Taffs were a bit short upstairs. Bloody good at rugby though, I'll give 'em that. And sing… oh, they can sing.'

Sugar laughed. 'They'll be bloody singing alright if they run into Wolf Man. Singing for their lives.'

Ten minutes later, the coach arrived at its nearest point, fifty yards from the wood. In the open field, Dracula led his flock to the fringe of the trees, shouting:

'We are here, Master! Your servants are here! Satan's children await you, here to do your bidding, to worship our beloved Prince of Darkness!'

*

Meanwhile, inside the wood, Bertie was busy repairing the cover of the wild boar pit, laying branches and leaves across it. He heard the Dracula party calling, now very close.

Dracula cried again: 'Oh Master, my Prince, show thyself!'

Baron Frankenstein muttered beside him: 'Maybe he's fast asleep. Could be he's not up until sunset.'

Suddenly Bertie broke cover. He howled:

'Hooooo-wooo-woooo! Kill, kill, kill! Bertie kill! My wood! I kill you all!'

The party turned and fled for their lives, sprinting out of the wood as if the devil himself was after them. They ran straight past their bus and into the gathering crowd of locals. Dracula, pale with terror, pointed towards the church.

The party made for it.

Father O'Conner, standing on the church steps, saw them coming. He hurried inside, slamming the door and locking it.

The group pounded on the door, shouting in unison: 'Sanctuary! Sanctuary! Sanctuary!'

From inside, Father O'Conner bellowed: 'Piss off, will yeh! You're not coming in here, yeh bunch of devil worshippers. So you can piss off, or I'll have the Lord strike you dead!'

Confused, the coach party then heard the bus horn: *Pap, pap, pap!*

They turned and made a mad dash for it. Owen sat waiting at the wheel as they tripped and fell over one another in the scramble. Dracula, knocked flat in the crush, was last to climb aboard.

Owen smirked. 'Err… where next, then? The Prince's grave at Whitby?'

Dracula, sweating and out of breath, snapped: 'Is one taking the piss, Boy-O? Back to Swansea, man. Back to some sanity!'

Chapter 24
THE KIDNAP

It was early evening on Pastures Road, a long stretch running just a few metres alongside Bogie Wood. On the road, a young lady was cycling. She wore a hooded cape and sang a French ditty as she crossed a small humpback bridge. Because of war restrictions, her headlight was shielded, casting only a faint light ahead.

Suddenly, the sound of a bell rang, followed by a clattering, then a scream. A startled partridge burst from the hedgerow. Pages from books blew across the road into the hawthorn. In the nearside ditch, the bicycle lay on its side, front wheel spinning, headlamp still glowing onto a trapped book. The cover read: Property of Miss Prudence Pringle.

Thirteen minutes later, Horace was guiding a frightened Pru into the cavern. She was tied, gagged and blindfolded. She struggled, trying to speak. Dora rushed to her, pulling down the blindfold and removing the gag before untying her. Pru blinked, adjusting to the light, then breathed a sigh of relief at seeing Dora.

'Dora! Thank God! What the hell's going on? Horace, you too—' She screamed on seeing Bertie wheeling in her bike and scattered belongings. 'Oh sweet Jesus… ohhh.'

Pru's eyes rolled back. She fainted.

Dora panicked, shouting at Horace: 'Water, clean water! She's in shock. Brandy – I need brandy. Wrap her up. Please don't let anything happen to her. Help her, Horace!'

Horace handed her a blanket and helped lift Pru into the armchair. They patted her hands and dabbed her brow. Slowly she stirred, opening her eyes. Dora smiled: 'It's me, Pru. Don't be frightened. You're safe.'

Then Dora rounded on Horace, kicking at him, and snarled at Bertie: 'Are you both completely mad? Bringing her here trussed up like a sack of spuds. You've gone and scared her half to death. Horace, I'm shocked. I'd have thought you'd know better.'

Bertie said sadly: 'Bertie wants sock.'

Dora frowned. 'Where's that?'

Bertie pointed at the sock lying at Pru's feet – the gag.

'Oh my God. How disgusting. Ooooww... Pru!'

Later, Pru sat shaken by the ordeal, only half-listening to Dora's attempts to explain. She glanced at Bertie in his tin bath and shivered.

Under her breath: 'This is absolutely ridiculous.'

'Did you say something, Pru?' Dora asked.

'Yes. You're in loads of trouble. The army, police ... everyone's looking for you. And now they'll be looking for me.' She gave Dora a sad look. 'Kidnapping...'

Horace interrupted: 'Pru, please forgive us. Believe me, taking you was our last chance. We need your help. If you don't want to, you can walk out and go home.'

Pru coughed. 'What's the matter with you two? Don't you realise the mess you're in? And now you're involving me. That's asking too much. Taking friendship too far, don't you think?'

Horace fetched the documents and pleaded: 'Just look through these, Pru. Tell me there's nothing unusual. If there's nothing to worry about, I swear I'll take you home first thing.'

She shrugged. 'What's to lose?' Fixing him with a glare:

'Don't forget, I'm holding you to that promise. No spies, and home for me. Agreed?'

'Agreed,' Dora and Horace said in unison.

Pru put on her spectacles and began reading.

'They're written in German. Addressed to someone called "the Shadow". It says: To the Shadow. Big sea bird flying on October 17th. Imperative that before you leave the house, you close the door. Leave nothing. Destroy.'

Bertie leapt from his bath, rifle in hand, pointing it at the cave roof. He danced and shouted: 'Big ducky coming! Bertie bang bang! Bertie's pot. Yum yum!'

Horace groaned: 'Not that kind of ducky, Father. A bloody seaplane, by the sounds of it.'

Pru whispered to Dora: 'He's never Horace's father, is he?'

Dora giggled. 'It's true, Pru. Who'd have thought? My father-in-law, the Wolf Man. Oops, language.'

Pru stared hard at them both. 'Horace. Bertie. You sure?'

Dora nodded. 'I'm afraid so.'

Pru shuddered, then continued.

'It goes on: All must be ready. Nothing left behind. The seabird will have no time to wait. And … something about jellyfish.'

Horace frowned. 'That it?'

Bertie rushed forward with a chunk of salmon. 'Man want jellyfish?'

Horace sighed. 'If you don't stop, I'll slap that salmon round your ears.'

Pru held up the papers. 'I think you're right. There are German spies in the area. And they want these badly.' She shook her head. 'I'll have to get back to school. My mum will be worried. She's probably phoned the police already.'

Horace hugged her. 'Thanks, Pru. Too late tonight, but we'll get you home before breakfast. Just wish I knew who this "Shadow" is.'

Pru leafed through the papers again. Dora sat blankly, Bertie hummed by the stew pot. Horace urged: 'Go through it all again, Pru. Step by step. Maybe we've missed something.'

An hour later, Horace sat in silence, still unsatisfied. Dora looked at Pru, hoping for answers. Bertie hummed as he stirred the stew. Finally, Pru waved her arms.

'It's plain as the nose on your face. Big seabird. That could only mean …'

'Big bird? Vulture!' Bertie offered.

'Ostrich!' he added.

Dora giggled. 'Don't be silly, Bertie. Ostriches can't fly.'

Horace cut in: 'No. But a great big seaplane can. It means airplane. A great big seaplane.'

Pru raised her thumb. 'Brilliant! Yes, Horace. A German seaplane, coming to take the spies and their information back to Hitler. Information to guide the Luftwaffe, to bomb our factories and docks. Stop production, and they win the war.'

Horace beamed. 'Well done, girl. I could bloody kiss you.'

Dora shot him a cold look, then smiled. 'I think I could kiss you too, girl.'

'Bertie too! Kiss Poo!' Bertie chimed in.

Pru groaned. 'If you don't mind, a thank you will suffice.'

Horace clapped. 'So, what did we have? This "Shadow" ran the show. He must have been desperate for the papers. Could he leave without them? Hard to say. One thing was certain: we had to get all this to the police, to the army. But how?'

The three fell silent. Dora shrugged. 'We'd think on it, love. I'd make us all a nice cuppa tea.'

Chapter 25
MAD HOUSE

In the asylum, night has fallen. Doctor Klinsmann's office sits empty, until the door flies open and Klinsmann storms in, followed by his assistant, Stephen Klaus. Klinsmann is furious. He tears off his overcoat, flings it to the floor, then skims his Homburg at the hat stand. It misses.

Klaus, clutching a new transmitter, looks terrified. In his heavy north German accent he stammers:

'The transmitter... where shall I put it, Herr Doctor?'

Klinsmann kicks his desk.

'Ver, ver... why not take it into the village and ask if they'd like a new transmitting machine, eh? Tell them the German Secret Service are here, giving them away for free!'

With one sweep of his hand he clears everything from his desk, fists slamming down as he snatches up the telephone. Resetting the receiver, he dials, drumming his fingers impatiently.

'Yes, Commander. It is me. We have a big problem. Serious, yes. Our operation in the barn has been infiltrated... the transmitter, gone. Klaus, his coat, his hat, gone. No news on the vehicle, the documents. Yes, I agree. We must leave. Of course. I will give the barn one last search. Let us hope.'

He shoots Klaus a glare.

'My assistant? Klaus is as much use as an ashtray on a motorbike, you can be sure. I will transmit from my office. Time is short. I will keep you informed. Heil Hitler!'

*

Back in the cave, Pru and Dora fiddle with the transmitter, running through frequencies. Horace watches Bertie polishing his boots with duck fat.

Suddenly, a voice comes through, in German. Dora points at the set, excited.

'That's him! That's Jellyfish, Horace. It's Jellyfish again!'

Horace races to the transmitter. Bertie looks for something to wipe his hands on and grabs a piece of floral material – one of Dora's dresses. She gasps as he smears it with grease.

'Shhh!' Pru hisses, scribbling notes.

The voice of Jellyfish drones on, then cuts out, replaced by music. Pru looks up, animated.

'It's important. Dora's right. Jellyfish was contacting the Shadow. He asked what had gone wrong, and whether there were copies of the documents. The Shadow replied it was the loss of the army vehicle. No way now to get the papers and maps to Zero Nine in France. But Zero Three has a copy, in Flamdale. He'll be bringing it personally on Sea Bird. The Shadow said by the eighteenth, the papers will be in Berlin.'

A heavy silence.

Horace shrugs. 'That puts a spoke in things. Flamdale… what's in Flamdale?'

Dora answers: 'Only that funny big house. The one for mental people. Nothing else.'

Pru nods slowly. 'Yes. The asylum. And come to think of it… its head is a German. Could he…?'

Horace jumps in: 'Be Zero Three? Aye, there's a thought.' He ruffles Bertie's hair, then sniffs his hand, grimaces, wipes it on his shirt. 'That's not got "Night in Calcutta" on it again, has tha?'

Bertie leaps for his rifle. 'I kill! I kill them all!'

Horace sighs. 'Tha'll take me to the edge of the wood and show me that barn. We know they've still got a transmitter. It could be there. I doubt it, but I'll give it another once-over. If I'm not back by midnight, you two get to the police station. Tell Ginger.'

Dora clutches his arm. 'Be careful, love. Don't let them Jerrys get you.'

*

In the Enfield estate barn, Klaus lies in the hayloft, half asleep. His greatcoat is buttoned to his chin, an empty schnapps bottle by his side. At a noise below, he rolls onto his stomach and peers through a crack in the boards.

The barn door creaks open. A woman pushes in a wheelchair, bumping it against a timber upright. A man's voice snarls:

'Get that lantern lit before I break me bloody neck, gal.'

The match flares. Babs Seymore, cloaked in blue, sets a lantern aglow. The light reveals an elderly man in tartan, deerstalker on his head, a blanket over his legs. Lord Enfield.

Babs throws back her hood, revealing little beneath. His Lordship hands her a picnic basket, rubbing his hands in anticipation.

'On that bench, Babsy baby. Let's get some snorter in us, warm the blood, eh?'

Babs giggles, wiggling her hips. 'I'm your kind of animal, you think you are…'

Lord Enfield licks his lips. 'Pour out the drinky-winkies, darling. Fuel the old body. Then, I've a little surprise for you.'

Babs pours champagne. He points at a pile of sacking in the corner. 'Under there. Go on. Look.'

She pulls it back to reveal a gramophone: *His Master's Voice*, complete with records. She squeals with delight.

Babs winds it, sets a record spinning. Music blares: *The Sheik of Araby*. She sways, hips rolling. 'Oh, one of my favourites.'

Lord Enfield beams. 'My maid used to dance like that for me. Sexy, like.'

'Bet you gave her pressies for it,' Babs teases.

'Aye, I did. I was big then. Big in all departments.'

She disappears into the shadows with a carpet bag, re-emerging scantily dressed in veils and fishnets. Twirling, shimmying, belly shaking, she sings: 'I'm the Sheik of Araby… dum-di-dum…'

'Off! Off!' His Lordship shouts, eyes gleaming. 'Let's see something!'

Above, Klaus gawps through the crack. *Must fetch the doctor… the thieves are here… but for how long?* He creeps to the loft hatch, fumbling onto the rope hoist.

Babs hears the noise. She freezes. 'What's that?'

'Owls in the loft,' Lord Enfield dismisses.

'Owls? Sounded like a bloody condor to me.'

Klaus slips. He crashes to the ground outside with a howl of pain.

'That your owl?' Babs hisses.

'Sounded like a stag in rut,' His Lordship chuckles. 'Lucky bugger. I used to sound like that in my prime.'

*

Horace creeps up to the barn, hugging the hedge. He sees Klaus limping away down the tractor path, then hears a motorbike start and fade.

Horace spots a ladder, climbs to the loft and peers through the boards.

'Chuffin' hell's fire,' he mutters.

Below, Babs twirls in veils, Lord Enfield rocking in his wheelchair, reaching for her. Babs swigs champagne, laughing: 'Makes me feel like I'm flying, like a bird!'

'Aye, and don't I know it,' he grins. 'Four bottles a week, baby doll.'

Babs sways closer, Lord Enfield sliding from his chair to his knees, arms wide. 'Baby! Gis a kiss, you bloody nympho!'

The record ends, leaving only the needle's scratch and their panting.

Suddenly car doors slam. Heavy boots thump.

The barn doors explode open. Klinsmann and Klaus stride in, black leather coats gleaming, pistols drawn.

From the loft, Horace gasps.

'Pissin' hell! It's them. The spies.'

PART FOUR

Chapter 26
SPIES

With Babs scurrying to pull on her clothes and Lord Enfield crawling back into his wheelchair, Klinsmann stood grinning, waving his pistol at them. He turned to his assistant Klaus, who was licking his lips at the scantily dressed Babs.

'What have we here, Klaus? Err, seems we have interrupted, how they say, shag-bang, eh?'

Klaus's eyes gleamed. 'Shall I shoot them, Herr Doctor?'

'I will shoot you in a minute, imbecile,' Klinsmann snapped.

Babs struggled to her feet and helped Lord Enfield into his chair. She shouted at the two intruders.

'What's wi all this chuffin gun-waving, eh? Who do you think you are? We're old enough. Consenting adults. What gives you the right?'

Lord Enfield snarled at the men. 'Yes. This is my land, my barn, and you two are bloody trespassing.'

Klinsmann twirled the pistol on his finger and turned on Babs. 'Shut it, you old sow. These guns give me the power to blow both of you away. Maybe I will do that. Yes.'

Lord Enfield shuddered. 'I don't know what you want from us. But look here, can't we work something out between us, if tha knows what I mean?' He nodded towards Babs and winked at Klinsmann.

Klaus began nodding furiously. Klinsmann punched him and smiled at Lord Enfield. 'Ha, ha. But you see, my fine friend, you are in no position for bargaining. It is I who is holding the cards, as you say.'

Babs shrugged. 'Alright, what's tha want? A tickle of me tits and then we go free?'

Klinsmann grinned. 'Oh, I will tickle your tits, alright. Yes, with my electro-probe. You wish for thrill? I will give you one you will never forget. One you can share together. I have many probes to give many thrills. Now we stop playing, how you say, silly buggers. You tell the good doctor where you have hidden my papers.' He shouted, 'My transmitter!'

He leaned over Lord Enfield, face to face. 'My papers. My transmitter. Where are they, you buffoon?'

Klinsmann pulled away and checked his watch. Babs and His Lordship only shrugged. His Lordship shouted back, 'We have no idea what tha's talking about … papers, bloody transmitters.'

Klinsmann looked at Klaus and drew a cutting motion with his hand. 'Enough!' He glanced at Babs and motioned at her scattered clothes. 'Best you get the rest of your rags on, eh? Quickly now. Dress, Frau, and do not keep the good doctor waiting.'

Babs pointed a finger and snarled. 'Why? We're not going. We want to stay here. We don't know ow't about thee bloody papers and transmitters. So why don't you two piss off and leave us be, eh?'

Klinsmann ignored her, grinding his teeth, and turned to Klaus. 'In the car with them. Take the man, dump the wheelchair. He won't be needing it if he's going. I will take the old Frau.'

Babs, still dressing, shot back, 'Hey, less of "old Frau". There's many a good tune played on an old fiddle.'

'Good,' Klinsmann said, winking. 'I will let all my crazy patients know this when I throw you to them.'

Klaus dragged the struggling Lord along the floor by his collar. 'The Shadow, he will be pleased, Herr Doctor.'

Klinsmann kneed him in the groin. 'You continue to use that loose tongue of yours and I promise you I will cut it out, idiot!'

'Sorry, Herr Doctor Klinsmann… ohhh,' Klaus muttered, in pain, but he kept dragging the lord.

Klinsmann booted the cowering Klaus and the terrified lord through the door. He shoved a frightened Babs after them and turned off the lantern.

In the upper hayloft, Horace crept to the doorway and peered out. Below, Lord Enfield was tied and gagged, then shoved into the back seat of the car. Babs, gagged with her hands tied behind her, was pushed into the front. Klaus bent to the crank, started the engine and the starting handle flew out of his hands, hitting Klinsmann.

Klinsmann hopped and shouted at the now terrified Klaus as the car lurched away. From the hayloft, Horace smiled and punched the air.

'Got yeh.'

One hour later in Bertie's cave there had been a long, heavy silence after Horace told them what had gone down in Enfield's barn. Horace sat with his arm around Dora, who was crying; Pru and Bertie, glum-faced, looked on.

Dora muttered between sobs, 'You're sure now, Horace? Sure that man, that Doctor Klinsmann, has got my mum and that Lord Enfield locked away in that funny hospital?'

Horace hugged her tighter. 'Don't worry, love. Babs'll be OK. This Klinsmann was grilling them about yon transmitter and those papers. They're bloody desperate for them.'

Pru said, 'This Klinsmann, Horace. He's not the Shadow, then?'

Horace shook his head. 'No, it's not him. But he, or she, is around here somewhere.'

Walking the Flamdale Asylum corridor, female attendant Nurse Greta Noss carried on her belt a large bunch of keys. She had just locked a room with the nameplate Bath House. She gave one last look through the small window, smiled with satisfaction and moved on, keys jangling.

A loud scream made her stop and return to the window. She peered in at a line of large wooden barrels standing upright. Heads poked through circular cut-outs; heavy padlocks fixed each most unusual "tub".

Of the eight barrels, six were occupied: Babs, Eric, Lord Enfield and three other male patients. Babs was shouting and arguing with Lord Enfield, while Eric stared in a catatonic state. In a corner a bald-headed patient wearing jam-jar-bottom spectacles appeared to be dead.

Noss smiled and slid the window cover shut. She looked at her watch, then strode down the corridor and through a door marked Staff Only. Inside, she sat for a moment gazing lovingly at a photograph of Doctor Klinsmann. She kissed it and slipped it into a locker.

Meanwhile, two doors down, Klinsmann reclined on a couch, a little intoxicated. A half glass of schnapps sat on the table. Strauss played from his new transmitter. He puffed on a Havana and conducted with the cigar.

The phone rang. He ignored it. It persisted. He groaned, staggered over and snatched it up.

'Yes? What is it? Don't you know vat time it is? Who is it? I am not pleased with this disturbance of my leisure time. So speak up. Who is it?'

In the Boggleswick police house, Ginger Perkins spoke into his phone. 'I have a special warrant issued by Police Headquarters in reference to your patient, Private Eric Swan. Can you hear me, Doctor?'

Klinsmann sighed. 'Can't this wait till morning? Swan is under sedation. At this moment the man is practically brain-dead.'

Ginger fired back, 'I shall have with me the most established Doctor Watson, who will be taking over responsibility. Doctor Watson has been commissioned by the army. We will be with you first light. Good night.'

Klinsmann stuttered, 'But he's not ready. He's a bloody cabbage, man.'

'But you have heard of our Doctor Watson,' Ginger said. 'He's very demanding and travelling from London. His time comes at a high cost, I'm afraid. Please do not disappoint us, Doctor. First light.'

Klinsmann slammed down the phone and screamed, 'English bastard!'

Ginger smiled and picked up his book: *The Hound of the Baskervilles*. He poured himself a glass of milk stout. 'I promised me sen I'd get thee out of yon nuthouse, Eric old son. Couldn't leave thee in there. Tha'd be dead in a week. Aye, and thee, Klinsmann ... well, I'm keeping a bloody eye on thee. Fancy thee knowing our Doctor Watson. Sir Arthur Conan Doyle'll be pleased.' He peered at the page. 'Where was I now...'

Back in Bertie's home, Horace paced up and down, deep in thought. Dora and Pru were still looking at the documents, while Bertie sat in his bath, trying – and, for once, succeeding – to clean his hands with petrol that Horace had drained from the lorry.

Horace glanced over as he passed. Bertie nodded, gave a weak smile and showed his hands.

Horace shook his head. 'When that's finished, take that can and them cloths outside. Tha's stinking place out.' He stopped, squinting at the rag Bertie was using. He went over, pointed and snarled, 'Bloody hell! That's one of Dora's blouses.'

Bertie leapt out of the bath and ran from the cave.

Dora shrugged. 'Don't be too hard on him, love. My mum could get just like him, a bit puddle-brain. Now she's in that horrible nuthouse.'

Horace nodded. 'Aye. It's not his fault.' He looked between the two women. 'Listen, you two. I've a plan. It's a risk, but right now I can't think of a better one.'

'Penny for your thoughts, Horace,' Pru said.

'Aye. Well, I'm saying it's a risk. I think you, Dora, must go with Pru tomorrow morning. Go see Ginger. Let Pru explain what we've found. Tell him about your mum and His Lordship. Tell him that Klinsmann and his crew are German spies. Don't say anything about me and Bertie and this here cave.'

Pru nodded. 'Yes. That's the only way. I can vouch for Dora. She's completely innocent in all this lorry business. Dora will be fine, I'm sure. Besides, Ginger Perkins has a bit of a soft spot for me, so he will listen, or feel my wrath.'

Dora bit her lip. 'You sure, Horace, love? Oh, what's gonna happen if you're wrong?' She looked to Pru. 'Pru, you sure about Ginger? I won't go to prison, will I?'

Chapter 27
BLACKPOOL

In the asylum courtyard, Eric sat drugged in the sidecar of a motorcycle combination. Klaus revved the engine, grinning, while Klinsmann and Nurse Noss stood watching. Klinsmann clamped his fingers in his ears and shouted:

'Will you stop revving that damned engine! Do you want all those nutters awake? Remember, take him far. I don't want to see Swan's ugly face ever again.'

Klaus throttled down, eyes gleaming. 'Can I take him to Blackypool, Doctor? Tower, lights, donkeys… always Klaus wishes to see.'

Klinsmann rolled his eyes at Noss, then snarled: 'Wherever, whatever, just get rid of the dog. And Klaus, remember, it's for the Fatherland.'

'Heil Hitler… err, Doctor.'

Klinsmann spun to check no one had heard, then snapped: 'Act like a buffoon again and the only light you'll see is the glow from the enemy's bullets.' He clasped his hands like a priest, glaring up at the sky.

Klaus, wobbling on the footrests, revved again. The bike lurched and he flew over the handlebars. Picking himself up, he avoided Klinsmann's murderous stare. Klinsmann drew his Luger in fury. Klaus scrambled back into the saddle, kicked the starter and rattled through the gates.

Klinsmann turned to Noss with a twisted smile. 'He's gone. Tell me he's gone, Noss. Two birds with one stone, eh?'

*

At dawn, the police house phone rang. Ginger Perkins, pouring his tea, picked up.

'Boggleswick Police.' He listened, frowning. 'Why, Doctor, I … What? Gone? Swan's gone? Escaped? Taken your assistant with him, last seen heading south for London? Aye, I'll put out an alert. Keep you informed. Good morning, Herr Doctor.'

He hung up, muttering: 'Herr Doctor, is it? We'll see about that.'

*

Back in his office, Klinsmann slammed down his phone with a grin.

'How's that, Constable Perkins? Something to worry about for that peanut of a brain. Thinking you could outsmart me.'

He yanked open the window and spat into the wind, only for it to whip back in his face. Spluttering, he bellowed to the morning sky:

'I will kill you, you interfering English bastard!'

*

At that same hour, Dora and Pru stood nervously outside the police house, wrapped in army cloaks. Dora scanned the empty street; Pru stamped her feet.

'Come on, Ginger. Get out of bed, lad.'

Dora whispered: 'Is he coming or what?'

The door opened. Ginger appeared, mug of steaming tea in hand. Pru snatched it from him and swept past.

'What the … who is it?' he barked.

The cloaked pair barged into his office. Pru shot the lock on the door.

'Hey! What you locking that for?'

The girls flung back their cloaks, half-dressed in army kit. Ginger gawped.

'Pru? Dora? What the hell's going on?'

Pru winked. 'Pour Dora a cup of tea, lad, and we'll tell you all.'

*

Meanwhile, back in the cave, Bertie returned from a pilfering trip, arms full of blouses. He laid them out proudly. Horace eyed the bundle, then spotted brown wrapping paper stamped:

To: MARI ROEBUCK BOUTIQUE, MARKET STREET, BOGGLESWICK, YORKSHIRE.

Horace sighed. 'That's not … bloody hell, you've half-inched from a shop now? Father, you've got to give this up.'

'Pressie for Dora,' Bertie said meekly.

Horace shook his head, then put an arm around him. 'Listen. Dora and Pru, they're not here. I've sent them to the village to tell the police about the spies. And you and I, we're going to the asylum. Big bird landing. We have to catch it. We can't let them take those documents out of the country. Understand?'

Bertie's eyes gleamed. 'I kill big bird. I kill mince spies. Jerry Germany. I shoot Shadow dead.'

Horace gave a dry smile. 'Aye, and that's why you're not having a gun. You'd shoot the lot of us. We're in a life-and-death situation, Father. You'd best remember that.'

*

One hundred miles away, on the edge of Blackpool, Klaus had pulled up at a roadside garage. He swung down from the BMW combination, Eric dozing in the sidecar.

113

'Two-stroke or four?' asked the pump attendant, shuffling over.

Eric cracked an eye. 'Err… two-stroke. Fill her up. He's got the lolly. Aye, he's got it.' He pointed lazily at Klaus.

The man filled the tank, watching Klaus wandering about, staring skyward. 'What's he looking for?'

Eric shrugged.

The man screwed the cap back and ambled over to Klaus. 'If it's the privy you're after, it's round back. Don't use too much paper, mind. It bungs up the drain.'

Klaus brightened. 'Bunged up, ah, yes! You bung us up. Tower!'

The attendant scratched his chin. 'Tower? Bung thee and him up tower?'

The motorbike roared to life. Eric, now helmeted, goggled and gloved, shot down the road in a spray of gravel.

Klaus spun, arms flailing. 'Please! Come back! You must obey me! Bring it back now! Oh, Doctor will shoot poor Klaus! I am dead, I am dead!'

He turned back to the old man, desperate. 'Please show me your bung-up Tower before I die.'

Chapter 28
SCOTLAND YARD'S FATS' ARRIVAL

It was noon in the police house and Dora, Pru and Ginger were sitting in his kitchen having a breakfast of egg on toast with non-steaming cups of tea. A prolonged silence hung in the room before Ginger, with a shake of his head, broke it.

'Well, what a tale. I'm speechless, to say the least. Bloody spies operating in our village. I felt there was something not right with that Klinsmann.'

Dora angrily stabbed a finger. 'Aye, and he's got my mum.'

He looked at them both, shaking his head. 'For a start let me say there's nothing I can do for Horace. His problem is with the army and not me. But I can promise you that I will put in a good word.'

He stood, walked to the window and looked down the street. 'I'm expecting some help from Scotland Yard. One of their top men is on holiday in Whitby and is coming to help out. I think that, along with Kennedy and Jack of course – your father, Dora – well, we have more than the makings of a good team. I will call for a meeting this very afternoon. We won't – can't – let them get away. So leave it with me.'

Pru gave him a peck on the cheek. 'We'll have a night out when it's all over. Dora will be stopping with mum and me. You have my number. If anything happens, let us know.'

They all suddenly jumped at a rat-tat on the door. The latch rattled up and down but it was locked. Ginger peered through the window. He saw a stoutly built man of about fifty eating a cream bun.

'I think it's him,' Ginger muttered, moving to the door. 'The detective... err, from the Yard.'

He opened the door and invited the man in. The man looked at the two girls, then at the breakfast table where several slices of toast remained. He selected a couple of slices and asked if there was any jam and if there was tea in the pot.

'Good day to one and all. Is the kettle on?'

Ginger made for the kettle but was blocked by Pru, who winked at him. 'I'll make tea. Does the gentleman – sorry, I didn't get a name – take milk and sugar?'

The man winked. 'That's because I didn't tell you. Three sugars in a mug, and milk. My name, by the way, is Rumble. Brian Rumble. But you can call me Fats... everyone else does. Chief Inspector Brian Rumble. That's what it says on the passport. Any buns? Nice piece of cake will go down with the tea, don't you think, ladies?'

Ginger smiled and offered Fats his seat. He went to a cupboard and brought out a large Bakewell tart, placing it on the desk. Fats's eyes lit up.

'Best I can do, Sir,' Ginger said.

Fats grinned. 'Yes, Constable. But what are you having, lad?' He let out a hearty laugh.

Dora interrupted, introducing herself. 'I'm Dora, and making the tea is Pru. You love your buns then?'

Fats nodded. 'Not half. Brought up on 'em. My dad had his own bakery in Whitby. So I lovingly blame him. What time's breakfast? Best meal of the day. Really famished this morning.

Could eat a bloody elephant, tusks and all.' He winked and nudged Ginger. 'Get a fry-up going, Constable. Make use of thee.'

He looked closely at the girls in their army attire, coat sleeves too long, trousers rolled up, boots oversized. 'You girls army, eh? Can't say much for how we're dressing our troops, especially ladies.' He waved a finger up and down at their uniforms.

'Would not have our police improperly dressed.' He looked at the tall figure of Ginger, cracking eggs into a frying pan. Ginger's trousers were too short, and he wore odd socks. 'Then again, we do look for our officers to be six foot or above.'

Dora contradicted him. 'But you're not six foot, Mr Rumble, are you?'

Fats shrugged. 'Ah well, I'm a little different, see. I'm what you might say from a special school, my good lady.'

Dora asked, 'What, like Pru?'

Fats looked at Pru, who tried to stop Dora saying too much. Pru shrugged. 'Yes, I went to a special school.' She looked daggers at Dora and through gritted teeth hissed, 'Didn't I, Dora?'

Fats nodded but seemed more concerned with Ginger's cooking. He was already on his third piece of Bakewell tart.

'Drop more tea, gal,' he said. 'I'm saying special school... you could say a school for thought, see. Oxford. They snap you up. The police, if you're an Oxford man you could be a little midget and they'd have yeh. Brains, see.'

Ginger turned. 'I like Sherlock Holmes.'

Fats scratched his chin. 'Sherlock Holmes? Who's he?'

Pru clapped her hands and, pulling on her cape, nodded for Dora to do the same. She patted Inspector Rumble on the shoulder. 'Nice to have met you, Detective Rumble.'

She pulled on Ginger's sleeve. 'Thanks, Ginger. I'm sure you'll put Fats – err, Detective Rumble – in the picture. We must go to my mum's; she'll be worried if I'm not back.'

She turned to Dora. 'So, come on, Dora, we have to go.' To Ginger she added: 'You will let us know about any further developments.'

Ginger asked, 'Do you want me to inform Jack, Dora... about Babs?'

Before Dora could answer, Pru jumped in. 'Err, no. Better not to worry him. If you do see him, you can assure him that Dora is safe and well.'

Pru took Dora's hand and dragged her out the door, shouting back: 'Byee!'

Fats looked at Ginger. 'What was that all about? Never mind. You can tell me over breakfast. Is it ready yet? I'm bloody starving.'

Ginger added mushrooms and bacon to the pan. He laid knives and forks on the desk and made to take away what remained of the Bakewell. Fats wagged a finger.

'Oh, you can leave that bit, Ginger old son. Bit of dessert after breakfast. It'll only go stale. My mum always had fresh every day. Bet your village has a lovely cake shop – cream buns, custard slices. By the way... what time's dinner?'

*

It was late afternoon on the deserted Boggleswick to Flamdale country road. From behind a dry-stone wall Horace's head appeared. His face was blackened and he was in uniform. He looked left and right along the empty road. Vaulting the wall, he raced across and dove head first into a gap in the hedgerow. His face reappeared, looking back.

'Come on then, what's tha waiting for? We ain't got all chuffin day.'

The blackened face of Bertie popped up, looking over. Horace waved him on. Bertie walked back, took a run and jump and went rolling head over heels into the road. Horace shook his head and looked skyward in prayer. Bertie sat rubbing his knee.

'If the good Lord happens to let us get through this day in one piece,' Horace muttered, 'then my cock's a bloater.'

He rushed out, grabbed the limping Bertie across the road and shoved him through the gap into a cattle field. A sign nailed to a nearby tree read: BRIDLE PATH TO FLAMDALE.

Horace smiled and winked. 'Good spotting, Father. This'll cut some miles off. By following this field it'll take us near to that Nazi Klinsmann.'

Bertie, hands on hips, shook his head.

'What the chuff's wrong wi thee now?'

Bertie pointed at the cattle, who had gathered in a group, staring. 'Not moo-moo cows. They bullies. They no titties.'

Horace gulped as the cattle began to move towards them. 'Yes, well… I think best we circle this field, Father.'

*

The light was fading; dusk approached. In his office Klinsmann tore up documents and threw them into the fire. He checked an open safe, found it empty and closed it. Then he heard crackling from the transmitter on his desk. He rushed over, fumbled with a dial and the static cleared.

A male voice, oddly feminine in tone, called: 'Big Bird calling, Big Bird calling Shadow. Come in, Shadow. Over.'

Klinsmann donned the headset, threw a switch and spoke into the microphone. 'Hello, Big Bird, hearing you loud and clear. This is Shadow's right-hand man… Zero Three. Over.'

In the cockpit of a German plane, disguised with painted red crosses on its fuselage, the pilot scanned the landscape. He wore a jacket with the badge of the Berlin Flying Circus, a well-known display team. Eating a crust with one hand, joystick between his knees, he worked the transmitter with the other.

'I hear you, Shadow's right-hand man. I am in need of instructions. I am a little lost. My compass has gone kaput. I really need you to guide me in, darling.'

Klinsmann almost tore his hair out. 'Lost? Darling? How the hell can I tell where you are? You idiot. Fly lower. Look out your window, man... Err, you are a man? Tell me what you see. Over.'

The pilot leaned out. 'Hello, Sweety. Can see twinkling stars. I think it's nighttime. No lights below me. Will go lower. Over.'

Klinsmann groaned. 'You are not related to Stephan Klaus, are you? I wouldn't be able to take it if you were. Listen to me. You must fly north, follow the big star. Look out for lights – a large circle of torches that I will light. The torches will be surrounding a lake. You will land your plane on the lake. You will get here on time or I will see that you are shot. Do you comprehend, Sweety? Over.'

'North. Yes, to my right. I see it, the big star. Yes, I see it. Over and out.'

He switched off, scratched his chin and muttered to himself: 'Some help he is. Bet he's awesome with a whip. Can't understand how he knows my cousin Stephan, though.'

*

Klinsmann sat at his desk cradling a quarter of schnapps. He drank deeply, sighed and set the bottle down. A knock sounded at the door.

'Enter.'

Noss entered, smiling, clicking her heels and saluting. 'We have secured all the patients, Herr Doctor. To your instruction the explosive charges have been set. The torches are lit. I have instructed our crew to make their own escape back to Germany. Will I be coming with you, Herr Doctor?'

Klinsmann finished the bottle and tossed it into a drawer. He shook his head. 'You have performed well, Noss. But alas, I cannot take you with me. You must set off the explosions. Blow this place and all in it to kingdom come. There must be no trace. Let the English bastards think we have all been annihilated, eh.'

Noss's face fell. 'But I thought—'

Klinsmann hugged her. 'I am so sorry, Noss. But…' He smiled at her sad face. 'I have arranged a pickup for you. A boat will be awaiting your arrival. You can take my car. Your contact's name is Reece. He's an undercover agent, working as a trawlerman. Don't worry, he's German. You will soon be back in Essen. Home.'

He held her hand and led her to the door. She sobbed. 'Thank you, Herr Doctor.'

Klinsmann went to the window and gazed at the torches glowing around the lake. He sighed. 'So sorry, Noss. You have been a good servant to me. But I must take orders too.' He shrugged. 'There is no agent Reece. I really do hope you make it home.'

*

Meanwhile, out on the Pennine road, Eric was driving the bike at full throttle. He passed a sign: WELCOME TO YORKSHIRE.

He grinned and shouted, his voice carried on the wind:

'I'm coming, Klinsmann. Bagley. Wolf Man. Eric's coming for yeh. Eric's gonna make you suffer. Yes… you're all going to die. Yeh set of baaaastaards!'

*

One hour later in the asylum bathroom, Babs and His Lordship were still in their bathtubs of cold water. Both were shivering. Three more zombified figures sat with them. The bath that had held Eric was now empty.

Babs, teeth chattering, moaned: 'Where the chuff is everyone? I'm chuffin freezing. Where's that bastard Klinsmann and that goon of his? I want the bloody toilet…' She began to scream. 'Help! Help!'

One inmate, eyes wild, growled: 'Shut it! Shut up, you stupid bitch. Shut that gob of yours or I'll steal your breakfast… and yeh dinner… and I won't let you play with my spiders.'

Another inmate stirred, one eye blinking rapidly, his head twitching. A voice came suddenly from another tub: 'That you, Kenny? Can I have my fluffy back? I know you got it. I ain't daft, yeh know.'

Kenny snarled and began to chant. 'Can't have it, can't have it, can't have it, can't.'

Lord Enfield roared: 'For God's sake, you thieving little bastard, give him his chuffin fluffy back! You hear me!?'

Babs joined in. 'I'll give him some bloody fluffy! Soon as I get free of this tub. Good kick in the bollocks is what Spider Man'll get from Babs. Will somebody let us out of here?'

Her shouting triggered voices from the corridors and cells: 'Out of here! Out of here! Out of here! Out of here!'

*

In the asylum pharmacy, Noss hugged a picture of a smiling Klinsmann, tears running down her face. Footsteps thundered closer. She quickly dried her eyes, straightened her uniform. The door opened and Klinsmann stormed in, angry.

'Noss, what is this commotion? A man can't think with this noise.'

Noss stroked his arm, gazing adoringly. 'Soon there will be one big noise, my Doctor, and all these crying maniacs will be blown to hell.'

Klinsmann shied away. 'No! No, you must not, Noss. You must release them all before the explosions. This must be done.'

Noss looked puzzled.

'Don't you see?' Klinsmann whispered. 'Letting them go will cause confusion. Can you imagine? These mad cretins running in every direction. What would this do for our escape plans?'

Noss smiled and winked. 'Why, they would cause such havoc... such distraction.'

'Exactly, Noss.'

She nodded. 'I see why you are such a champion, my Doctor.

Why, you would make those English idiot pig-dogs think that the nutters had blown this place, and us along with it.'

Klinsmann smiled, lightly kissed her cheek and walked out.

The chanting and screaming rang in his ears as he strode the corridor. He stopped, shouting: 'Just keep it up! Just keep it up! There will be no supper tonight. No rice pudding!'

There was a sudden lull. Klinsmann smiled to himself.

Chapter 29
A DAY OF RECKONING

In the police house Ginger was cooking a rabbit stew. Fats was looking at maps of the area while eating a cream bun. 'How's the supper coming along, Ginger? Smells good, especially when the old belly's rumbling and the stomach thinks me throat's cut.'

Ginger wiped the sweat off his brow, tasted his creation and nodded. 'I'll give it a few more minutes, Sir. Rabbit's done, carrots still alive... a bit hard.'

Fats put the maps to one side and gave his belly a rub. 'Gives a man thinking power, does a full belly. Funny, but I've never got around to solving a case without me belly full. There was this murder once, aye, happened in a London restaurant. Solved it in three weeks... never left the scene of that crime.'

He sniffed the air and rolled his eyes. 'Should be done now. Don't matter if carrots are a bit hard. Let's get some food into us. Bloody long day tomorrow.'

Ginger began to plate up.

'Oh, and Ginger, best we let the army take charge of any mistakes. It'll be on their necks, not ours. Early breakfast, full fry-up. Make sure that gets them bag o' buns from the cake shop. And make sure they're fresh, not yesterday's. We don't want bellyache eating stale buns.'

*

Later that afternoon in the asylum grounds, lakeside, Horace crept around following the path of the burning torches. He threw a wet blanket over one torch, putting it out. He turned to see Bertie following, relighting the torches he had extinguished.

'Can tha, before I lose me temper, tell me why tha's lighting the torches when I've put 'em out?'

Bertie looked down, mumbling. 'Not good… can't see. No light.' He pointed to the sky. 'When big bird comes, big bird no see.'

Horace sighed. 'Aye, that's the whole chuffin idea.'

Bertie scratched his beard. 'Bird no see, bird no land. Bertie can't catch Jerry Germans. Bertie can't kill Klinsmann. No bird, no Shadow come.'

Horace nodded. 'Sometimes tha knows a little bit of sense comes into that squirrel brain of thine. So good thinking, Father. For once tha's right.'

Horace took the torch off Bertie and relit the one he had just extinguished. He then scanned the area for somewhere to wait, pointing to a nearby boatshed. He walked towards it, waving for Bertie to follow him.

The shed doorway was open to the lake. A covered rowing boat was tied there, sitting in the still water. They pulled back its cover and climbed in. Pulling the cover back over them, they relaxed and waited. In no time at all they were both fast asleep, snoring.

*

Earlier, on the Boggleswick to Flamdale road, villagers, army, police and home guard were marching to Flamdale. They passed a sign that told them they had only a mile to go. Sergeant Major

Kennedy strode ahead, followed by Fats who rode on a shire horse led by the local coalman, Wally Slack. Wally was still black-bright, his horse Dobby shagged out and snorting. Fats, on his back, sat eating a bun.

Suddenly the sound of a drone from a plane's engine filled the air. They all looked up.

Ginger pointed at the sky. 'Faster, lads! That's the seaplane!'

Wally shook his head. 'My Dobby can't do faster than he's doing. He's a bloody coal horse, not Hyperion.'

RSM Kennedy shouted, waving his baton. 'Take cover, lads! That plane could have guns and bombs!'

The party all raced for the cover of the hedgerow, some getting spiked and tangled in hawthorn. Fats was left sitting alone in the centre of the road. Wally cowered under a bush, shouting out:

'Gerroff me hoss! I don't want him shot. Gerr him under yon tree out of the chuffin way.'

Scobie rushed out, shouting: 'Gi' him a few digs in his ribs with thee heels! Ain't tha ever rode a bloody horse?'

Wally snarled. 'Aye, I've seen them he's rode. All bow-legged in t'nacker yard. What he needs is a bloody elephant.'

Fats groaned. 'Can someone please hold me bun while I dismount? And don't you be nibbling at it either.'

*

In the plane's cockpit, dawn had broken and the pilot looked down on the circle of torches burning all around the lake. He pushed down on the joystick, lowering the plane onto its target. He skimmed across the water, looking out for a safe landing stretch. At the end of his run he spotted two figures on the bank waving their arms. One held a torch, waving it from side to side.

The pilot smiled and shouted: 'I see you, Shadow and Right-Hand Man. With names like that, we could become friends. I would introduce you to my friends at my club, The Crazy Sexy in Hamburg. Oooow, I like it. You call me Franz Klaus an idiot. I will show you, right-hand, just how good a pilot you call idiot. How good I fly my plane. So good, I shall land it so close my props will dry your hair and you will not get those toes of yours wet.'

Waiting on the lakeside bank, Bertie put down his torch and grinned like a cat with cream.

'Plane driver, he see Bertie. He wave.'

Horace nodded. 'Aye, Father. Let's just hope we're the only bods he's waving to. Remember, he's German looking for Germans. Probably one of the bastards bombing Sheffield. God help us.'

Bertie snarled. 'Bertie kill plane driver. He be very dead Jerry.'

The plane circled back, lowering again. Horace muttered: 'He's either gonna land, thinking we're his German brothers, or give us a burst of machine-gun fire.'

The aircraft skimmed the lake and landed perfectly. With propellers still twirling, it turned and taxied towards them.

The two quickly slid down the bank into the water. Horace landed on a clump of reeds; Bertie missed and ended up waist-deep.

'That was some five-star landing, that was,' Horace said. 'Just who is this guy, the Red Baron?'

He pulled Bertie up onto the reeds, whispering: 'This is it now, Father. And don't thee dare utter a chuffin word.'

The plane drew nearer. The pilot waved. Horace kept his head down, waved back and motioned for Bertie to do the same. The engine kept running as the aircraft came alongside. After a moment the pilot threw out a short ladder and encouraged them to climb.

Horace climbed first, Franz supporting him by the arm. The pilot noticed the uniforms. He spoke in German.

'We must vacate immediately, to get rid of those pig-dog uniforms. There is much activity on the outer roads. They're very close. I will give them fire on our way out. You can be sure I am a very good marksman, Herr Shadow... right-hand man?'

Horace, who did not understand a word, cried out: 'Arrrrgh, arrrgh!' Pretending an injury to his knee, he winced.

Franz patted him on the shoulder. 'Oooow, felt that myself, Sir. Are you good, not hurt yourself, Sweety? Let me give you a hand.'

The unsuspecting pilot held out his hand. Horace grabbed it and hurled Franz over the climbing Bertie into the lake.

Franz splashed, screaming: 'I don't like water! I am drowning! I can't swim! Why do you do thhhhhhis?'

He saw Bertie's growling face, the man licking his lips. Terrified, Franz screamed louder, splashed to the bank and scrambled up. He didn't look back as he scurried into the woods.

*

In the front courtyard of the asylum, Klinsmann was leaving with a briefcase in hand. A tearful Noss stood at the entrance watching him go. He stopped and turned, shouting:

'Remember, Noss. You must wait until we are airborne before the fireworks. Set the simpletons free, then boom! Boom! Yes! Safe journey. Reece. Cleethorpes.'

He waved a flapping hand.

'It is done. Good luck, Doctor.'

She sighed. 'I love you,' she whispered.

*

Some twenty minutes later, on the lake's far side, two figures sat in a rowing boat. One was Klinsmann, rowing. The other sat with his back turned, directing the cursing doctor towards the aircraft.

'Only a complete idiot would land on the far side of the lake,' Klinsmann muttered. 'How does our Führer expect to win this war with such imbeciles in uniform? Beats me.'

*

At the asylum gates the marchers reached the end of their weary trek. Kennedy halted the party.

'Remember, lads and lasses. When we get in there, spread out. We have no idea what to expect, only that inside lies one great enemy of our nation. Nobody leaves that building. Shoot anyone who attempts to pass. Don't let these rats escape you.'

Dora and Pru rushed forward to consult Kennedy. Dora, concerned, gave him a hateful look.

'Not my Horace you don't. You mustn't shoot my Horace.'

Kennedy coughed. 'Aye, Bagley... err, just bloody arrest him.' He looked at her, shaking his head. 'Still some unfinished business with him, Mrs Bagley.'

They all turned at the sound of Eric's motorbike tearing up the road. He drove the combo straight at them. They dove and fell in all directions. Wally's horse, Dobby, with Fats aboard, bolted like a racehorse, Wally chasing after. Fats held on for dear life, still clutching his bag of buns.

Eric roared up the main driveway. Inmates ran wild, some dancing with glee, all in striped nightshirts and barefoot. Some shuffled like zombies.

Noss was attaching a coil of cable to a power box. She turned and froze as the motorcycle approached fast. She held up a hand, signalling stop.

Eric skidded the combo to a halt, nearly overturning. He revved angrily, eyes scanning. Grinding his teeth, he growled at her:

'Where's that bastard Klinsmann?'

Noss shook her head, snarling: 'Where's Klaus? What have you done to Stephan, you crazy English pig?'

Eric revved, rolling the combo closer. 'I shall not ask again. Where is he?'

Noss's eyes flicked towards the lake. Eric caught her glance, nodded and smiled. He turned the combo, pointing it lakeward.

'I will be back for you,' he snarled.

At full speed he shouted: 'Eric is coming for you, Klinsmann. Be ready to die, for I will kill thee. Cut thee up into little pieces!'

Chapter 30

SWAN LAKE

Eric could see two figures in a rowing boat making for a waiting seaplane with its propellers turning. Klinsmann was puffing and panting as he rowed closer, pausing to wipe sweat from his brow. His companion wafted a finger, urging him on.

Klinsmann gasped. 'We shall soon be gone from this accursed country. I see the plane is well disguised. Painting the Red Cross was a brilliant idea. I'm sure you thought of it, Commander?'

They then heard the roar of a motorbike, faint at first but growing louder, with the screams of the pursuing Eric carrying over the water. The commander held up a hand for Klinsmann to stop rowing. Klinsmann obeyed, resting the oars. Eric's voice came over the water.

'Eric's coming, Klinsmann! A watery grave for you... food for the fishes!'

The commander's finger wafted urgently again, urging the doctor to row. Klinsmann snarled. 'It's that nutter Swan. I should have finished the man when I had the chance.'

Suddenly there was a great explosion. Smoke and flames rose from the crumbling asylum grounds. The army, police, home guard and villagers fell into disarray.

Fats clung for dear life as a revitalised Dobby went wild-eyed, crashing through hedgerows and fences. The horse stopped dead at the water's edge, hurling Fats into the lake.

'Aaargh! Ginger, help! Get me out, I can't swim! Where's me buns?' Fats flapped and spluttered. Ginger, Bobby and Percy rushed to his aid and dove in, only to find the water no more than four feet deep. Cursing, they hauled him out.

Percy, rubbing his head, glared at Fats. 'Yeh great lump o' lard. What a pillock.'

Their faces turned to horror as Eric roared towards them on the combination like a rodeo rider. They sank back into the lake up to their necks.

With a huge leap Eric took the combo over their heads into the water. He flew off at the last second and struck out, swimming like an Olympian after the boat. Between strokes he shouted:

'Eric's coming to get yeh! You won't escape Eric boy!'

Fats blinked. 'What the— Who the hell was that?'

Ginger nodded towards the swimmer. 'That, Sir, was our Eric Swan.'

Behind them, the asylum burned into ruins, smoke and dust filling the sky. Most inmates danced and laughed in joy at their release, pawing and tickling each other.

Through the smoke Kenny, Spider Man, staggered, carrying a struggling Babs over his shoulder. He licked his lips and laughed while Babs screamed:

'Jack! Jack! Where's the chuff are yeh? Come n' get this crazy bastard off me, Jack!'

Kenny mimicked her. 'Jack, come see Kenny's spiders!'

On the driveway, Lord Enfield limped on crutches, pursued by a man in striped pyjamas clutching a flower. The man called in a high-pitched voice:

'Wait for me, baby! Lola won't hurt you. I could be your lady. I've never had a lord!'

Lord Enfield snarled back: 'And I've never shot a man, but if you don't piss off, you'll be the bloody first! So piss off!'

By the lakeside, Fats, Ginger, Bobby and Percy stood soaked, watching Eric swim with tireless fury towards Klinsmann's boat.

Fats pointed. 'So that's the man? Eric, the army failure?'

Ginger nodded. 'Aye. A broken man. But he certainly hates Klinsmann.'

Bobby shook his head sadly. 'He's lost it. Gone totally mad.'

Percy added: 'Mad, aye, but he'd make a cracking soldier. Born leader, that man. Just mad.'

Ginger raised his field glasses. 'Two in the rowboat. And Eric's closing on them. Wonder who the other one is…'

He saw Klinsmann stop rowing and draw a pistol, firing four rounds. Eric ducked underwater at the first shot. The commander grabbed Klinsmann's arm, holding him back. A strong male voice barked: 'Row.'

The boat rattled against one of the plane's floats. Klinsmann and the commander clambered up the ladder and inside. The commander yanked it from Eric's grasping hand and slammed the door.

'They're inside. Eric's locked out, stood on the ski! He'll get himself shot, the bloody fool,' Ginger muttered, lowering the glasses.

A disturbance came from behind. RSM Kennedy, face blackened and blistered, uniform torn and smoking, ran past them and dove into the lake.

In the cockpit, Bertie sat in the pilot's seat, helmet and goggles on, Horace beside him with a pistol across his knees. Klinsmann stormed down the aisle, shouting:

'Get moving, man! Have you fallen asleep? Get us in the air, you idiot! Can't you see we're surrounded?'

Bertie began to rise, but Horace pushed him back down, shaking his head. Outside, Eric clung to the plane's ski, beating his fists on the undercarriage and shouting over the roar of the props:

'Open this door, Klinsmann! Face me, yeh piece of pig shite! Eric'll gi' thee bloody shock treatment!'

Klinsmann turned his pistol on Bertie. 'You will get this plane up now or I'll shoot you where you sit. Your co-pilot will take over.'

Bertie fiddled with the levers and throttle. The plane jolted forward. Horace whispered: 'Chuff me, Father. I didn't know you could fly.'

Bertie gave a weak smile. 'Don't tell me tha' chuffin can't... oh my God.'

He yanked the joystick. The plane lurched into the air, throwing Klinsmann and the commander to the floor.

From the lakeside, Ginger watched through the glasses as the plane kangaroo-hopped across the water, finally lifting off. Eric still clung to the strut, battling the slipstream.

'He won't last,' Ginger muttered, handing the glasses to Fats, who seemed more concerned with his missing buns. Percy pointed to waterfowl pecking at an empty paper bag.

'That's lost 'em, old cocker.'

Fats sighed. 'Me buns... the greedy little chuffs.'

Eric edged along the float to a window, banging his fist on the glass and gasping for breath.

'Klinsmann... you'll not get rid o' me. I'll follow you to Berlin. These hands... round your neck...'

Inside, Klinsmann stumbled to his feet. 'What are you doing, you imbecile? Fly this plane home safely!'

He strode to a hatch, pistol in hand. 'I'll finish this Swan once and for all.'

Horace rose, his own gun trained. 'I don't think so, Doctor. If anyone's finished tonight, it's you, and your Shadow.'

Klinsmann froze and dropped his weapon. The commander stood, rubbing his neck.

'Private Bagley,' he sneered. 'The cause of all our problems. The army won't believe you. They'll believe me, Colonel Harris.'

At that moment, Eric's face appeared at the window. 'Bagley! Son of Satan! A traitorous German!'

Harris levelled his gun at Horace. 'Hand it over, Bagley.'

Horace passed his pistol to Bertie, who fumbled with the joystick. The plane jerked. Harris and Klinsmann tumbled, their guns sliding across the deck. Horace snatched them both.

'Tie them up,' he ordered. 'The army will see who the real traitors are.'

Eric, outside, screamed through the glass. 'It's him! The Wolf Man! The devil himself!'

Below, Ginger shouted a warning as something fell from the plane.

'Bomb! Take cover!'

They all hit the dirt. Moments later Eric came whistling down, screaming, and crashed into the lake.

The aircraft zigzagged above, circling a reservoir. Klinsmann and Harris sat bound back-to-back. Horace kept watch with a pistol, while Bertie, half-asleep, struggled to keep the plane steady.

Horace prodded him awake.

Chapter 31
THE DAM

S omehow the plane managed to make it to a suitable landing site: a long waterway that was part of the great northern reservoir system. Kennedy and Ginger had commandeered a Flamdale horse-drawn fire engine. Immediately behind came a busload of army, home guard and Boggleswick locals, including Babs, Dora and a worn-out Fats. The bus bore the words *FLAMDALE ASYLUM* on its side. All were staring skyward, following the plane.

*

Horace nudged Bertie's shoulder. 'Hope tha can land this bloody thing, Father.' He pointed to the fuel gauge. Its needle sat on empty. 'Because we're near on dry.'

Bertie shrugged. 'No petrol juice. We land like ducky on water.'

Horace grimaced. 'I didn't think we'd hang in the air flapping these wings like a chuffin' skylark. Tha's got to get us down on yon water, OK?'

Klinsmann, white-faced, snorted. 'Jesus Christ! That idiot will kill us all. He has no idea how to fly a plane... we must do something, Commander.'

The engine coughed, spluttered, then died, the plane beginning to lose height. Klinsmann began to sob. 'I will never see my beloved Mutter again… my little dog Gunter…'

Harris snarled. 'Shut up, you whimpering fool. You are German. Die like one, if need be.'

*

At the southern end of the man-made dam, a large open marquee overlooked the holding wall. Inside, comfortably seated, were officers of His Majesty's Royal Air Force, along with Winston Churchill and arms engineer Barnes Wallis.

Churchill was explaining to Wallis. 'You see, Barnes, my dear chap, the problem is not bombing these German dams that supply the Ruhr industries – the Möhne, Sorpe and the Eder dams – but getting our aircraft safely out and back home. The dams are heavily protected. That would result, as you well know, in our boys getting a lot of flak from mounted machine guns. That's to—'

He stopped. His cigar nearly fell from his lips as a seaplane came into view, skimming the surface. The officers gaped as it made a miracle landing, bouncing across the water before coming to rest against the dam wall.

'What on earth!' Winston exclaimed.

The party stood and stared, mouths agape, at the procession approaching. Kennedy, astride the fire engine, was saluting furiously. Behind him, the busload of villagers and soldiers waved enthusiastically.

Churchill turned to his officers. 'I shall want a full report on this… err… leak in security.'

One RAF Air Marshal muttered, 'Just a local fire practice by the look of it, Sir.'

Churchill jabbed his cigar at the bus. 'Ruddy police and army driving a fire engine, followed by a busload of nutters. Are they taking the piss or what, Air Marshal?'

The officers followed his gaze to the bus, where Jack Seymore was leaning on the horn with relish.

Barnes Wallis pointed towards the lake. The plane's crew were emerging. Churchill clapped Wallis on the back, then punched the air.

'Well, I'll go to my mother's! What a cracking demonstration, Barnes. I congratulate you, my dear fellow. A ruddy first-class show, old boy!'

He pressed one of his special cigars into Wallis's hand. 'You certainly kept that under your hat… a bouncing bomb, eh? Well done.'

Wallis laughed awkwardly. 'Err… ruddy bouncing bomb… yes, Winston. But the plans need a few more days to refine.'

Everyone crowded around him, offering congratulations. One Air Marshal nodded. 'Spiffing good show! Liked the way you used one of the enemy's crates and not one of ours. Good painting the Red Cross on it. If you hadn't, one of our lot would've brought her down, what!'

Wallis scratched his head. 'Yes… it was good. Yes.'

Churchill was escorted to his car. He turned, wagging his cigar. 'The crew – I want them decorated. Risked their lives, they did. See that for me, won't you?'

His aide nodded briskly. 'Think of it as already done, Sir.'

Chapter 32

THE HERO'S RETURN

One week later, Boggleswick village square was decked in flags and bunting. A large crowd had gathered. A long banner was stretched between two telegraph posts. It read: *HORACE BAGLEY OUR HERO*.

Up on a wooden platform, a row of chairs had been set for family and the Lord Mayor, the Right Honourable Norman Piggot, who sat centre stage. To his left sat Babs and Jack Seymore, Ginger Perkins and Fats Rumble. Fats was eating a large apple slice. To Norman's right were two vacant chairs, then May and Dora Bagley and Pru Pringle.

Standing to one side with a megaphone was Captain Strong. The restless crowd began to whistle. Strong raised his arm and spoke through the horn.

'Now, now, is that the way to welcome our hero home? After being cleared of all criminal charges, and, might I add, decorated? Surely a moment to treasure and remember on this great day.'

A voice from the crowd shouted, 'Where is he then? Where's Horace? We've come to see our Horace!'

Tony Cantaloni shook his head. 'Are you going to get this going before my ice cream melts, ah?'

Fats whispered to Ginger, who nodded. He turned to Tony and asked, 'Err, Tony, could you give Inspector Rumble a large bowl full?'

Tony shook his head. 'He must pay for what he already had. He owes me eighteen shillings. He never pays. Says put it down on your bill. If you pay, then Tony give, OK?'

The crowd fell quiet as the sound of a brass band flowed into the square. The band marched down Main Street playing *Onward, Christian Soldiers*. Behind them walked Horace, smiling and waving with one hand while in the other he firmly gripped a struggling Bertie. A cardboard box sat on Bertie's head, two eye slits cut out, but the box had shifted, and Bertie could not see.

'Bertie can't see! Bertie blind!' he mumbled.

Horace turned the box around. Bertie's eyes flashed through the holes. 'Bertie sees now. Bertie no like people. Bertie wants go home.'

'Bertie's going home,' Horace told him. 'Tha's got a big surprise coming, tha has.'

The band struck up *The Floral Dance*. The seated guests rose, clapping the arrival of the pair. Horace led Bertie to his seat next to May, who tried to edge away. Horace gave May a peck on the cheek and whispered,

'It's a surprise, Mum.'

May, somewhat alarmed, answered, 'Oh, Horace love, you know how I hate surprises.'

Dora squeezed her hand. 'Oh, this is a lovely surprise, Mum. You're going to love it.'

The Lord Mayor addressed the crowd, then sat. The crowd began chanting for Horace. Captain Strong motioned him forward. Horace waved and bowed, then spoke.

'Thank you, everybody, for this nice reception you gave me. Aye, but yeh must remember, I couldn't have done it alone. Not wi'out me beautiful wife Dora and our good friend Pru. It was every bit a team effort, and those spies are no more. I gave the police information and I've heard today that the one called Klaus was caught while climbing the tower in Blackpool. The other, the female Noss, was found soliciting in Cleethorpes. The pilot, a one-time member of a group calling themselves The Gay Cavaliers, a German flying acrobatic air team, well, he was arrested while asking for sanctuary at Whitby church, of all places.

'As fer the main instigators, Flamdale's Doctor Klinsmann and the traitorous Colonel Harris – the one known as the Shadow – I'm told sentencing will be made by a future court martial. Harris is looking at a death sentence.'

The crowd cheered. Horace raised his hand in appreciation.

'Thanks, but now it's time to introduce the other part of my team, with a special surprise for me mum.'

Horace grabbed Bertie's arm and stood him before May. The crowd gasped, eager to see the man under the box. A hush fell as Horace whipped it off.

Babs screamed, pointing at Bertie. 'That's him! The Wolf Man! He's the chuffin' Wolf Man! Jack, bloody kill the bastard!'

Bertie cowered, ready to run. Horace held him tighter. The crowd began to mutter angrily. A man shouted, 'Yeh, that's him all right. Satan himself! Needs a silver bullet to kill him.'

Suddenly a gunshot rang out. Ginger had fired into the air.

'Now listen here, you lot. It's Horace's day, and I for one am thankful for what he's done. So shut yer gobs and let's hear what he's got to say.'

The crowd fell uneasy but silent. Horace nodded his thanks to Ginger, then turned to May, arms outstretched.

'Well, Mum?'

'Well what, son?' she asked, puzzled.

'Has he altered that much in twenty-five years?' Horace pressed.

'Has who altered, love?'

Horace pointed at Bertie. May took out her spectacles. Bertie gave a wide, toothless grin and began jumping up and down. He rushed to hug her.

'My May, my girl May. Bertie's girl… my girl.'

May hit him with her handbag. 'Gerr off me, I aren't your girl!'

Horace jumped between them. 'Chuffin' hell, Mum, don't be too hard on him.'

May, wiping her brow, snapped, 'Don't be hard on him? It's thee I ought to be hitting. Fancy digging yon bloody nutcase up!'

Horace sighed. 'He's been living in a chuffin' cave for twenty-five years. That's what's sent him nuts. He's still me dad.'

May laughed. 'Thy dad? Him? That bloody nutcase? Tha thought he was thy dad?' She chuckled, clinging to Dora, who shrugged at Horace.

The crowd roared with laughter. Bertie seized the chance and bolted.

'He's not me dad? Then who is he!?' Horace cried.

May, tears streaming with laughter, replied, 'He's thy father's old Romanian gypsy mate. Old bozz-eyed Bertie Bostock.'

Horace gaped. 'Not me dad, Bertie Bostock?'

He turned to see Bertie fleeing up the road, heading for Bogie Wood. He shouted after him: 'Boooosssstokkk!'

May, weak with laughter, leaned on Horace. 'They had him locked away in yon asylum, love. Escaped, come to think of it, about the time thy dad joined up. It was said he'd interfered wi' sheep. Aye, that were Flamdale, before Jerrys moved in.' She grew serious. 'Sorry, love.'

Horace's face fell. 'Not me dad. Thought he were alive, I did.'

May touched his arm gently. 'Sorry, son. But thy dad's dead. Died in France, a hero. That's something to be proud of.'

Horace looked after the running Bertie and snarled. 'Yes, and I know someone who'll be joining him. Bostock!'

He leapt down from the platform and tore off after him, shouting, 'Bosssstokkk!'

They raced through the village, heading for Bogie Wood.

Meanwhile, approaching from the wood's edge, Eric marched quickly towards the square, face grim and eyes blazing. He muttered, 'Oh, Eric's coming for you, Bagley. No escape this time. Eric's a medals.'

Eric slowed as a figure ran towards him. The moonlight lit the runner's face. Eric rubbed his eyes, disbelieving.

'Noooooooo! It's him!'

He panicked and ran, crashing through a broken hedgerow into long grass. Bertie chased him, while Horace thundered after them, still bellowing, 'Boooooossssstttttoooookkkkk!'

Eric, crazed-eyed, stumbled in terror as Bertie closed in. He dove into the grass, Bertie pouncing after him. Horace followed. All three vanished, the sounds of a brutal struggle rising into the moonlit night: groans, screams, then silence … before a long, bloodcurdling howl.

Horace and Eric staggered back into view, torn and battered, faces twisted in terror. They screamed at each other, then staggered away in opposite directions.

From the long grass, another shape emerged: Bertie, wolf-like, growling, saliva dripping from his teeth. He held up his medal to the moon and howled.

'Owwwwwoooooo!'